BAKER STREET BOYS

Anthony Read studied at the Central School of Speech and Drama in London, and was an actor-manager at the age of eighteen. He worked in advertising, journalism and publishing and as a television producer before becoming a full-time writer. Anthony has more than two hundred screen credits to his name, for programmes that include *Sherlock Holmes*, *The Professionals* and *Doctor Who*. He has also written non-fiction, and won the Wingate Literary Prize for *Kristallnacht*.

The Baker Street Boys books, *The Case of the Disappearing Detective* and *The Case of the Captive Clairvoyant*, are based on Anthony's original television series for children, broadcast by the BBC in the 1980s, for which he won the Writer's Guild TV Award. The series was inspired by references to the "Baker Street Irregulars", a group of young crime-solvers who helped the detective Sherlock Holmes in the classic stories by Sir Arthur Conan Doyle.

For the Blagden Bunch and the Lewis Lot

THE CASE OF THE
CAPTIVE
CLAIRVOYANT

ANTHONY READ

Illustrated by
DAVID FRANKLAND

WALKER BOOKS
AND SUBSIDIARIES

LONDON · BOSTON · SYDNEY · AUCKLAND

First published 2006 by Walker Books Ltd
87 Vauxhall Walk, London SE11 5HJ

4 6 8 10 9 7 5 3

Text © 2006 Anthony Read
Illustrations © 2006 David Frankland

The right of Anthony Read and David Frankland to be identified as author and
illustrator respectively of this work has been asserted by them in accordance with
the Copyright, Designs and Patents Act 1988

This book has been typeset in Cochin

Printed and bound in Great Britain by J.H. Haynes & Co. Ltd

British Library Cataloguing in Publication Data:
a catalogue record for this book
is available from the British Library

ISBN-13: 978-0-7445-7016-8
ISBN-10: 0-7445-7016-6

www.walkerbooks.co.uk

CONTENTS

ONE

Sparrow was happy. In fact, he was so happy that
he had to keep pinching himself to make sure he
was awake and not dreaming. Only a few days earlier, Mr Trump, the manager of the Imperial Music
Hall, had fired him from his job as call boy and
general dogsbody. It was only a part-time job, helping out when the theatre needed an extra pair of
hands, but to Sparrow it was a passport to paradise,
a doorway to a magic kingdom. When he was
dismissed, he felt as though his whole world had
collapsed. He would have been inconsolable if he
had not been so occupied with other things.

It was those other things that had lost Sparrow
his job. He had been fired when a stage magician
had accused him of trying to steal his secrets – an
unforgivable sin in the theatre. But those secrets had

helped Sparrow and his gang of young friends to foil a deadly plot to murder not only Sherlock Holmes, the great detective, but also Queen Victoria herself.

Sparrow and his friends were street urchins, all either orphaned or abandoned, who lived together in a secret cellar which they named HQ, short for headquarters, just off Baker Street in London. They called themselves the Baker Street Boys – although in fact three of them were girls. Sparrow was the youngest and smallest of them all apart from Rosie, the flower girl, who was a bit shorter than him but probably slightly older. Only probably because few of the Boys were sure about exactly how old they were.

The Boys supported themselves by doing a variety of jobs, such as holding horses' heads for their owners to stop them straying while their carriages were parked at the kerbside, or by shining people's shoes, running errands, sweeping horse droppings from street crossings, selling flowers or newspapers, or, in Sparrow's case, helping out backstage at the Music Hall. But their most important occupation, under their leader, Wiggins, was helping Sherlock Holmes with his investigations.

It had been while they were assisting Mr Holmes that Sparrow had got into trouble at the theatre. But after they had saved his life, and that of the Queen, Mr Holmes's friend Dr Watson had called on the theatre manager and, after swearing him to secrecy, explained that Sparrow was a hero and must be given his job back at once. So now here he was, walking through the familiar door that led to the backstage area, the happiest boy alive.

"Wotcha, me little cock sparrer!" Bert, the stage doorkeeper, greeted him as he entered. "Nice to 'ave you back again."

"Ta, Bert," Sparrow replied with a broad grin. "Nice to be back."

"Learned your lesson, 'ave you?"

"Oh, er, yeah. Yeah, I s'pose so."

"Never thought Mr Trump'd take you on again. Comes of havin' friends in high places, eh?"

"I dunno what you're talkin' about."

"No?" said Bert. "Ain't no secrets from old Bert in this 'ere theatre. I knows everything and don't you forget it." He pushed back his official peaked cap and tapped the side of his bulbous red nose. "Ears like a hawk, me."

"I thought it was eyes what a hawk had."

"Yeah. Eyes and all." Bert nodded, blinking through his thick, steel-rimmed glasses. "'Ere, you better put this on and get started."

He reached back into his cubby hole and produced the call boy's jacket. Sparrow grabbed it eagerly, pulled it on and fastened the many buttons on its front, excited and proud to be wearing it again. He sniffed hard, taking in the familiar smell, a combination of dust and canvas and paint and hot lights and make-up, which to him was better than any perfume. Then he took a deep breath and pushed his way in through the swing doors.

He had barely taken two steps when he found himself facing the imposing figure of Mr Aloysius Trump, resplendent in his tailcoat and white bow tie.

"Ah, Sparrow," Mr Trump harrumphed, stroking the sharp point of his waxed moustache. "Kind of you to honour us with your presence."

"Yes, sir, Mr Trump. Here I am, back again."

"Like the proverbial bad penny."

"Beg pardon, sir?"

"That's what they say, Sparrow, my lad. A bad penny keeps turning up."

"Oh. Right."

"I hope you realize," Mr Trump went on, glaring down at Sparrow with one eyebrow raised menacingly, "what a serendipitously fortuitous juvenile you are?"

Sparrow looked blank.

"You're a lucky lad," Mr Trump translated, with a heavy sigh. "Affirmative?"

Sparrow gulped and nodded.

"Oh, yes, sir. Thank you, sir."

"Now then, young man, just listen to me. Out of the kindness of my heart and contrariwise to my discriminatory sagacity, I have graciously assented to reinstate you in your pre-existing position. But it is incumbent upon you to appreciate that this is by way of being a probationary appointment. Understood?"

Sparrow shook his head, gawping at him in bewilderment. Mr Trump bent down until his face was level with Sparrow's and spoke quickly and quietly.

"You can have your job back, but you're on trial. Put one foot wrong, and you're out on your ear. Got it?"

Sparrow grinned. "You can rely on me, guv'nor."

"Just don't upset the artistes, right? Especially Stanley the Strong Man – he can bend iron bars with his bare hands. Or Marvin the Mystic – he's got psychic powers. You never know what he might do to you. Turn you into a real sparrow and set the cat on you, I shouldn't wonder." Chuckling at the thought, Mr Trump turned on his heel and marched off through the pass door into the auditorium.

In an instant Sparrow was back in the old routine. He hurried around the dressing rooms, asking the artistes if they needed anything. He brought them refreshments from the theatre bar to lubricate their vocal chords, and sandwiches and buns to keep up their strength. He reminded them when they were due on stage. And as each one started, he took a large card with the number of the act and placed it on an easel at the side of the stage so that the audience knew who they were watching and who would be on next.

Sparrow loved the hustle and bustle backstage, the good-natured banter of the "artistes", as the performers liked to call themselves. He loved their gaudy costumes, their garish make-up and their nervous excitement as they waited to go on stage. He loved the sound of the band from the orchestra pit on the other side of the big red velvet curtain, the rattle and boom of the drums, the tinny blare and deeper oompahs of the brass instruments, the screech of the strings and the tinkling of the piano. He knew that as orchestras went, the Imperial's band was not particularly good. But, like the artistes, it was loud and lively and it suited the brash vitality of the music hall perfectly. Most of all, though, Sparrow loved the sound of the audience, laughing, singing along and enjoying themselves. Their applause, he thought, was the best music of all. One day, he told himself, it would be played for him.

The evening passed quickly for Sparrow as he scurried around behind the scenes without a moment to spare. He had no time for more than a quick glance at most of the acts. He managed to catch a brief snatch of song from Madame Violetta, the operatic soprano, which was so shrill it gave him a pain in the head. He saw Stanley the Strong Man heave one enormous weight above his head, and

Signor Macarelli the Knife Thrower start to pin his plump wife to a board by flinging stilettos across the stage. He caught half a joke from Cheerful Charlie Chestnut, the cockney comedian – it sounded like a good one but he would have to wait until the next night to hear the punchline. Then, almost before he knew it, it was time for the last act: Mystic Marvin and Little Mary.

Marvin and Mary had stayed in their dressing room with the door closed, so Sparrow had not seen them until they were ready to go on-stage. When he caught sight of them, he was quite bowled over. Marvin was nothing unusual: a sharp-faced American with a thin moustache and slicked-back dark hair. But Mary was a golden-haired vision, no more than thirteen or fourteen years old. Sparrow gazed at her as she stood waiting to go on-stage, nervously smoothing her red velvet dress, and thought she was the most beautiful girl he had ever seen. When she turned her wide blue eyes on him and gave him a small smile, he felt his cheeks burning into a deep blush.

While Marvin and Mary went through their act, Sparrow stood at the side of the stage, enthralled.

He watched wide-eyed as Marvin went through the motions of hypnotizing the girl, taking a small golden locket from around her neck and swinging it gently to and fro before her eyes.

The mystic turned to the audience and raised a finger to his lips. "Ladies and gentlemen," he announced. "I must ask for complete silence while I induce an hypnotic trance in Mary. Any disturbance at this time – any disturbance whatsoever – could be highly dangerous to my little girl."

The audience, usually so boisterous, became so quiet that every tiny sound was magnified. When someone coughed, all those around him hissed "Sssshhhhh!" – though this made a louder noise than the original cough. Even the bored barmaid at the back of the stalls stopped serving drinks and clinking glasses. Marvin turned back to little Mary, sitting upright on a small golden chair in the centre of the stage, and began swinging the locket again, like a pendulum.

"Now, Mary, my dear," he intoned. "I want you to focus on this locket. Clear your mind of everything else … everything … let it go completely blank. Your eyelids are getting heavy … heavy …

they are drooping … you are going to sleep … sleep … sleep…"

The girl's eyes closed, and her head dropped onto her chest. She was breathing deeply, as though fast asleep.

"Are you asleep, Mary?" Marvin asked.

"I am asleep, master," she replied in a strange voice.

Marvin turned to the audience and bowed slightly. There was a ripple of uncertain applause. He raised one hand to stop it, then drew a long, shiny hatpin from his lapel and held it up. Moving swiftly across the stage, he walked down the steps, approached a large lady sitting in one of the front seats, and handed her the pin.

"Madam," he said, "would you care to test this pin? See if it is sharp?"

The woman felt the tip, tried it carefully on one fingertip, and let out a little "Ouch!" before nodding vigorously and handing the pin back to him.

"Thank you, madam," Marvin said. "Don't worry," he joked as he bounded back onto the stage, "the bleeding will cease shortly."

Raising one of Mary's hands, he held up the pin

and plunged it into her palm. Or at least, that was how it looked to the audience, who let out a collective gasp of shock. From his position at the side of the stage, however, Sparrow could see that the pin did not pierce Mary's skin at all, but slid harmlessly up between Marvin's fingers. So it was no surprise to him that the girl felt no pain, or that there was no blood to be seen when Marvin apparently withdrew the pin and held up her unblemished hand for all to see.

Sparrow grinned when Marvin claimed that this proved Mary was now in a deep trance and ready to continue with a demonstration of mind-reading. Since this was the last act of the evening, the young call boy had time to stand and watch as Marvin covered Mary's eyes with a blindfold, then climbed down into the audience. From the top gallery of the theatre, a spotlight picked him out, following him as he moved up the aisle between the rows of seats.

"I am now about to demonstrate to you the amazing powers of mentalism," the American announced. "If someone would care to hand me an object – any object that you have about your person – I will endeavour to transmit its image to my little girl, who cannot possibly see what it is, except through the marriage of our two minds."

A ginger-haired man in a green suit took a fountain pen from his pocket and passed it to Marvin, who held it aloft so that everyone could see what it was before closing his eyes and pressing the fingers of his other hand to his temples.

"Are you ready, Mary?" he asked.

"I am ready, master," the girl replied mechanically.

"Right, then. Concentrate your thoughts... Can you tell me what this object is?"

Mary frowned under her blindfold, paused dramatically, then said, "I believe it is a pen. Yes, it is a fountain pen."

There was a burst of applause. Marvin acknowledged it, then went on collecting other things, all of which Mary identified correctly. Coins, watches, rings, handkerchiefs, wallets – nothing defeated her. She could even tell the difference between a copper penny and a golden sovereign.

Sparrow knew that it must be a trick, but he couldn't see how it was done, only that it was done very well. His admiration for the girl grew – not only was she pretty, she was also a real artiste!

Which made him all the more surprised when, passing her dressing-room door after the show, he heard her sobbing her heart out.

He was just about to knock on the door when Sparrow felt a heavy hand on his shoulder. It was Marvin, glaring at him angrily.

"Hey, you!" Marvin snarled. "Whaddya think you're doing?"

Sparrow staggered as he was pulled violently away from the door.

"Nothin'," he stammered. "I just wondered if you or Miss Mary needed anythin'."

"Why?"

"That's my job."

Marvin glowered at him for a moment. "We don't need anything," he snapped.

"Is there something amiss, Mr Marvin?"

Mr Trump had suddenly appeared behind Sparrow, looking threateningly at him. "Is the boy bothering you?"

"Nah. No problem."

"I'm pleased to hear it. The performance was extremely satisfactory tonight. Please accept my congratulations."

"Sure. Thanks. Now pardon me, but we gotta be somewhere else." He flung open the door and shouted, "Mary! Get out here now!"

Mary emerged from the dressing room, wearing a hooded velvet cloak over her stage costume. She was dabbing at her red eyes with a tear-soaked handkerchief.

"Oh, my!" Marvin shook his head at her. "Just look at you!"

He looked towards Mr Trump and sighed, "Kids!" Then he grabbed Mary's arm and hustled her through the stage door. "C'mon," he hissed at her, "we got work to do."

Sparrow watched them go, then looked up at Mr Trump.

"I reckon there's somethin' wrong there," he said.

Mr Trump frowned. "If there is, it's none of your business. Don't forget what I told you. One mistake, and you're out – for good."

Sparrow nodded glumly, but as Mr Trump marched away he hurried to the swing doors, pushed them open a little way and looked out. In the street he could see Marvin pushing Mary into a smart carriage that stood among the hansom cabs that were always waiting there to pick up the artistes and whisk them off to other theatres: some of the more successful ones performed at two or three theatres each night and needed fast transport to get them there in time. As the carriage moved off, the gaslight from the street lamp picked out something bright on its side. A simple monogram, painted in gold. It was the letter "M".

Two

"Moriarty!" exclaimed Wiggins, his eyes shining with excitement.

The other Boys, sitting around the big table in HQ, gasped at the name. Professor Moriarty had been the criminal mastermind behind the plot to murder Sherlock Holmes and Queen Victoria: Mr Holmes had described him as "the Napoleon of crime". What could he be doing with Marvin and Mary?

"We don't know it's him," Queenie, the oldest girl in the gang, said. "Not for sure. After all, Marvin's name starts with an 'M', don't it?"

"Queenie's right," Beaver agreed, sucking his big front teeth thoughtfully. "Could be his own carriage."

"Nah." Wiggins dismissed the idea. "He don't make that sort of money. I mean, the Imperial's not bad, but it ain't exac'ly the Alhambra nor none of them other fancy gaffs in Leicester Square, is it? No offence, Sparrow…"

Sparrow looked up from the plate of Queenie's stew that he was ravenously devouring for his supper and nodded. As always, Wiggins's reasoning was excellent.

"None took," he mumbled through a mouthful of potato and gravy. "You're right, he ain't such a big star. Leastwise, not yet."

"Nor will be," Shiner butted in, "even if he has got Goldilocks makin' eyes at all the blokes."

"She don't!" Sparrow snapped back, stung. "She ain't like that."

"Sure and what is she like then?" Gertie teased him, her green eyes twinkling. "Sugar and spice, and all things nice?"

"She's … she's lovely," Sparrow stammered.

"He's stuck on her!" Shiner crowed. "Sparrow's got a sweetheart!"

The others laughed as Sparrow blushed crimson, though Rosie, who was sitting next to him, put her hand on his arm and gave it a reassuring squeeze.

"You pay no heed to 'em," she told him. "Ain't

nothin' wrong with havin' a sweetheart."

"But I ain't," Sparrow protested. "She's just a nice girl what I think is in trouble."

"She is if she's in the clutches of Moriarty," Wiggins said.

Queenie held up a hand. "Hold on, we still don't know that," she said.

Wiggins delved into one of the pockets of his baggy old coat and produced a stub of pencil. Concentrating hard, his tongue sticking out the corner of his mouth, he drew a curly "M" on the table top.

"Was it like this?" he asked.

"That's it!" Sparrow cried. "Exac'ly!"

Wiggins sat back, grasped the lapels of his coat in his two hands like a lawyer and nodded solemnly. "I rest my case," he said.

Sparrow tugged at the brass bell pull by the shiny, black front door of 221b Baker Street. He grinned at Wiggins and Beaver as they heard the jangle of the bell deep inside the house, then the sound of hurrying footsteps, before the door was opened with a flourish by Billy, the pageboy. Billy, who was about the same age as the Boys, was employed by

Mr Holmes's landlady, Mrs Hudson, to admit visitors and run messages for her and her tenants. The expression on his shiny face swiftly changed from a welcoming smile to something like a sneer as he saw who it was.

"He's not here," he told them in a superior voice. "Mr Holmes is away on important business."

"We got important business," Wiggins replied. "We got important information for him."

"What he'd want to know about," Beaver added.

"Oh, yeah?" Billy replied. "How d'you know he would?"

"'Cos it's about—" Sparrow began to blurt out, before Wiggins stopped him by clapping a hand over his mouth.

"It's too important for you to know," Wiggins told Billy. "If Mr Holmes ain't here, we'll have to tell Dr Watson. You can announce us, if you please."

"Can't."

"Why not?"

"Because he ain't here neither. I mean," he corrected himself, switching back to his posh voice, "he isn't here either. They've both gone to Devon. Some trouble with a dog on Dartmoor."

❀   ❀   ❀

Back at HQ, the Boys held what Wiggins called a council of war, to decide what they should do next. Queenie was all for going to Scotland Yard, but Wiggins said Inspector Lestrade would never take them seriously.

"He did last time," Beaver said.

"And he knows the Professor was behind it all," Queenie added.

"Yeah, but we had Dr Watson with us then," Wiggins replied. "And we knew a lot more. Now we don't really know nothing."

"We'd better find out then, hadn't we?" Queenie said.

"How we gonna do that?" Beaver asked, scratching his head.

Wiggins turned his eyes to Sparrow. All the others did the same. Sparrow swallowed hard, then nodded.

"All right," he said. "Leave it to me."

"We will," Shiner grinned. "You're the one what's sweet on Little Mary."

Sparrow dived at him, fists flailing, but Beaver grabbed them both with his strong arms and easily held them apart.

"Now then, now then!" Queenie scolded. "Behave yourselves, both of you. We're here to fight criminals, not each other."

"Evenin' Mr Marvin, Miss Mary."

It was the next day and Sparrow had been hovering inside the stage door, waiting for them to arrive whilst trying to keep out of the way of Mr Trump, who seemed to suspect he was up to something. At last they appeared and Sparrow greeted them with a smile. He was rewarded with a warm smile in return from Mary, although Marvin just nodded curtly.

"Anythin' you need," Sparrow chirped, "just give me a call. 'Cos I'm the call boy, don'cher know?"

Marvin said nothing, but Mary smiled kindly at his little joke.

"Anythin'," he continued, looking hard at her, willing her to understand. "Sparrow's the name. Don't forget, now."

Before Mary could respond, Marvin took hold of her arm and steered her away to their dressing room, closing the door firmly behind them. Sparrow stood in the corridor, wondering what he could do now. How would he ever get to speak to Mary on her own when Marvin never let her out of his sight?

As the show progressed, and act followed act, Sparrow was kept busy. But all the time, as he dashed about, fetching and carrying and changing the programme cards, he managed to keep an eye on the dressing-room door. It remained firmly closed, and he was beginning to despair when Bert stuck his head through the swing doors and beckoned him over.

"Message fer Mr Marvin," he said, handing him a stiff white envelope and jerking a thumb over his shoulder. "From the gent outside."

As Sparrow took the envelope, his fingers felt something raised on the back. He turned it over and discovered an embossed monogram on the flap: the familiar curly letter "M". Peering past Bert, he shivered with excitement as he recognized the carriage waiting in the street beyond the stage door. He was brought back to earth by a sharp word from the doorman.

"Go on, lad! Jump to it!"

Sparrow didn't need telling twice. Clutching the letter as though afraid it would fly out of his hand, he trotted down the corridor and knocked on Marvin's door.

"What is it?" The American's voice sounded cautious.

"Message for Mr Marvin."

The door opened just a couple of inches, Marvin peered suspiciously through the crack, took the envelope from Sparrow, then closed it again. A moment or two later, he came out of the room, closed the door carefully behind him, and hurried through the stage door to the street. As soon as he had gone, Sparrow knocked quickly on the door and, without waiting for an answer, slipped inside.

Mary was sitting at the dressing table, wearing her stage costume. To Sparrow she looked prettier than ever, but her face was sad. She let out a little cry of alarm as he entered.

"It's all right," he reassured her. "It's only me."

"What d'you want?"

"To help you."

Her lovely face looked even more miserable and her golden curls trembled as she shook her head.

"You can't. Nobody can help me."

"Yes, I can. Me and my friends can. We're the Baker Street Boys – we can do anythin'."

"Anything?"

"Anythin'." He leant forward and whispered confidentially, "We saved Her Majesty the Queen from being murdered. Only don't tell nobody – it's a deadly secret."

Mary's eyes opened wide as saucers.

"Could you help me escape from *him*?"

"From your dad?"

"He ain't my daddy. He's my stepfather, and I hate him."

"Right. Yeah, course we can."

"I'm desperate to get away from him. Only, I got no place to go and I don't know anybody in England."

"You do now," Sparrow told her. "I'll have a word with the others tonight, and we'll make a plan."

"You really think your friends would agree?"

"Sure as eggs is eggs."

"I mean, they don't know me, or nothing about me."

"No, but I do. And when I tell 'em, they'll all want to help you. Just you wait and see."

"That'd be just wonderful." Her eyes filled with tears, but this time they were tears of happiness. "Oh, Sparrow, I could kiss you!"

Sparrow backed away hastily. "Just be ready tomorrow night," he told her. "And leave everythin' to me."

"Leave what to you?"

The harsh voice came from the doorway. Sparrow spun round to see Marvin glaring at him. He thought fast.

"Oh, hello, Mr Marvin," he stuttered. "I was just askin' if Miss Mary would like some pop."

"Pop?" Marvin rasped.

"Yeah, you know. Lemonade, or dandelion and burdock—"

"Dandelion and...? What you trying to do, poison the girl?"

"No, sir. It's real good is dandelion and burdock. Very refreshing."

"Get outta here. And stay out. We don't need nothing."

He gave Sparrow a violent push, sending him

reeling into the corridor. As the door slammed behind him, Sparrow heard Marvin say, "You better be on your best behaviour tonight. The professor's got another engagement for us. A real important one."

Back at HQ, Sparrow recounted all that had happened.

"I still dunno what he's up to," he told the other Boys, "but it's gotta be no good."

"Pity you couldn't have read what was in that note," Wiggins said.

"I would've, but the envelope was stuck down," Sparrow explained.

"You could've steamed it open," Shiner said.

"Yeah, the geezer I used to work for did that," Beaver joined in. "You hold it over a boiling kettle and the steam melts the glue, then all you gotta do—"

"I hadn't got no kettle," Sparrow interrupted him. "And anyway, I didn't have no time."

"Course he didn't," Queenie said, giving Shiner a withering glance. "Stupid idea."

Shiner shrugged – he was used to his elder sister putting him down. "Bet there was one somewhere in the theatre," he argued. "Else how could they make a cup of tea?"

"Shiner! Shut up!" Wiggins told him sharply. "We got some thinking to do."

"Like how in the name of all that's holy are we goin' to rescue that poor little spalpeen from her wicked stepda'?" Gertie asked, sounding more Irish than ever as she scratched her ginger head.

"And from Professor Moriarty," Beaver added.

"Precisely," said Wiggins, in his best Sherlock Holmes manner. "Don't forget the wicked professor. There could be some danger if he's got anything to do with it."

"Don't we know it," Queenie said.

The others were silent for a moment as they remembered their last encounter with Moriarty.

Then Sparrow piped up. "I don't care about danger," he said defiantly.

"Nor me," said Rosie, and the others all joined in. Only Shiner said nothing – he was still sulking after being told to shut up.

"So," said Wiggins, "we're all agreed – we're gonna help Mary? Right. Then we'd better start making a plan."

*   *   *

They spent the rest of that night and most of the next day working out what they were going to do.

"First thing," Wiggins began, "we gotta get Marvin outta the way."

"How we gonna do that, then?" Beaver asked.

"It ain't gonna be easy," Sparrow said. "He don't never let her outta his sight."

"Poor girl!" Gertie sympathized. "Fancy havin' a da' like that – even if he ain't her real da'."

"'Specially if he ain't her real dad," Rosie added.

They sat and thought, pummelling their brains as they tried to find an answer. Wiggins paced up and down the room until his face suddenly lit up.

"Moriarty!" he exclaimed.

"What's the professor got to do with it?" Shiner asked.

"Everything!" Wiggins replied. "Think of the note. That got him outta the door, didn't it?"

"Yeah, but…" Beaver looked puzzled. "How we gonna get the professor to send him another?"

"We don't need to. You're gonna call at the stage door and say you've got a message for Mr Marvin. You say there's a gent sitting in a carriage round the corner as wants a word with him."

"What gent?"

"There ain't no gent, you dope. But Marvin'll think it's Moriarty, won't he?"

"Oh, right. So he'll go out round the corner to look for him…"

"Exac'ly! And while he's gone, Sparrow nips into the dressing room and gets Mary out to the rest of us."

"Brilliant," said Beaver, looking impressed.

But Queenie had her doubts. "And what happens if Marvin turns round and comes right back," she asked, "and the first thing he sees is Sparrow bringing Mary out?"

The other Boys had to admit that this was a problem. Sparrow said they didn't have to bring Mary out through the stage door. She could climb out of the dressing-room window into the alleyway at the back of the theatre. But Marvin might still see her making her escape, and give chase. They needed more time. How could they get it? How could they get Marvin far enough away from the theatre so that he would not see Mary leaving?

It was hours later that Wiggins and Queenie

came up with the answer, with a little help from Sparrow.

"Got it!" said Wiggins. "To start with, she don't come outta the theatre. We just make Marvin think she has, but really she's still in the dressing room. Sparrow can hide her somewhere, then leave the window open so it looks like she's gone out that way."

"Brilliant!" said Beaver again. "So he goes chasin' off lookin' for her…"

"And when he does," Sparrow said, "I get her outta the window for real. Yeah, brilliant!"

"'Cept Marvin will be out there lookin'," Shiner reminded them.

"You're right," Queenie acknowledged grudgingly. Shiner grinned at her, pleased that for once she agreed with him.

This called for more hard thinking. But eventually Queenie had a bright idea. "If I was to disguise myself as Mary, I could get him to chase after me and lead him in the wrong direction," she said. "He could end up miles away while the rest of you bring her back here, safe and sound."

"Brilliant!" said Beaver.

"But what if he catches you?" Rosie asked, worried.

"What? Catch me? Round here?"

"Fat chance of that," said Wiggins. "And even if he did, what's it matter? He'll only discover he's got the wrong girl."

"Brilliant," Beaver repeated, mightily impressed.

"But how you gonna fool him?" Shiner persisted.

"Easy," shouted Sparrow, caught up in the excitement of the plan. "Mary wears this red velvet cloak when she comes to the theatre, and it's got a hood what you can pull over your head!"

"Perfect!" said Wiggins. "Queenie waits in the alley behind the dressing rooms. When Marvin goes lookin' for Moriarty, Sparrow passes the cloak out through the window, then leaves it open while Mary hides. Then Queenie makes sure Marvin catches sight of her running away, and Bob's your uncle!"

Next day, Sparrow was at the theatre early, eager to alert Mary to the plan. Wiggins and Beaver took up positions outside the stage door, ready to play their parts in spiriting Mary away, while Queenie hid in the alley. They had a long wait because Marvin and Mary were the last act on-stage, but the Boys were too excited to mind.

Sparrow, who was busy looking after the other artistes, did not see them until they were in their dressing room and so couldn't tell Mary about the plan, or warn her to be ready. So it came as a surprise to her when he slipped into the dressing room while Marvin was out looking for Beaver's imaginary gentleman, and told her it was time to escape. But her reaction came as an even bigger surprise to him.

"Escape?" she asked, staring at him blankly. "Why?"

"From Marvin. Quick – hide!"

"Hide?"

"Yeah. From Marvin!"

"I cannot leave Marvin," she said, in a strange, flat voice. "I have to stay with him and keep the secret."

"But you said…" Sparrow stammered. "I got it all fixed."

"I don't know what you're talking about." She shook her head, looking puzzled. "You better get outta here before Marvin comes back. He don't like me talking to strange people."

"Strange people! Us?" Queenie exclaimed crossly. "Cheeky madam."

Sparrow sat hunched over the table at HQ, quite despondent, as he finished telling the others exactly what had happened. They were all indignant.

"If you ask me, it's her that's the strange one," Gertie said.

"I nearly froze to death hanging about in that alley waiting for her." Queenie held out her hands to the stove, to warm them.

"Made a real charlie outta you, didn't she!" Shiner taunted Sparrow.

"Never mind, Sparrow," Rosie comforted him. "We still love you."

"It weren't your fault," Beaver added. "Let's forget all about it now."

He patted his stomach and looked at Queenie. "We got any cocoa left in that tin you found?"

"That's a good idea," she replied. "Who's for cocoa? Wiggins?"

Wiggins had been pacing the floor again, deep

in thought, while the others were talking. Now he stopped and held up one hand.

"There's something very funny about this," he announced.

"Yeah, I'm killing myself laughing," Queenie said with heavy sarcasm.

"I mean funny peculiar," Wiggins retorted. "How could she forget, when she'd been so upset? She might have changed her mind, p'raps, but not forgot all about it. What's this secret of Marvin's, what she's gotta keep? And what's it all got to do with Moriarty?"

"I dunno. What?" Beaver asked innocently.

"That, my dear Beaver –" Wiggins sounded more like Sherlock Holmes than ever – "is what we are going to find out."

THREE

"Why didn't you come for me?" Mary hissed at Sparrow as he passed her dressing room the next evening. "You promised."

Sparrow was taken aback. "But I did," he protested.

"I trusted you," she continued, almost in tears. "You said you and your friends would help me."

"We would have done if you'd let us."

"What are you talking about?"

"We had everythin' fixed. But you wouldn't come."

"What?" She stared at him, puzzled. "I don't understand."

"No, nor me neither."

Sparrow had been nervous of approaching her, afraid that she would rebuff him again. But she had called out to him as though last night had never happened. She was the same girl as she had been two days before, and Sparrow's heart melted once more.

"I don't know what's goin' on," he told her, "but if you still want us to help, we're all ready to give it another go tonight. OK?"

She nodded vigorously. "Oh yes. Yes, please."

Before Sparrow could say any more, he heard Marvin's harsh voice from behind him in the corridor. "'Yes please' what? Is he trying to poison you with his dandelions again?"

Sparrow spun round and forced a smile on to his face. "Evenin', Mr Marvin," he said cheerfully. "Dandelion and burdock ain't so bad, honest. You oughta try it."

"I told you before," Marvin said, "she don't need nothing. So scram."

Sparrow kept smiling, saluted and left, but not before whispering urgently out of the side of his mouth to Mary: "Be ready!"

For the rest of the evening Sparrow hopped about the theatre like a cat on hot bricks, trying to do his job and keep one eye on Marvin's dressing room at the same time. He was waiting for Marvin to leave the room long enough so that he could slip inside. Although the other Boys had decided they would try once more and were all in place outside, they couldn't use the same trick as the night before – Marvin had been furious when he'd discovered there was no one waiting for him, and he would certainly not fall for it again. All they could do was look out for a suitable opportunity.

Sparrow was beginning to lose hope as it got nearer and nearer to the time when Marvin and Mary were due on-stage, and still the mystic stayed put behind the closed door. Salvation finally came from the most unlikely source: Mr Trump. He knocked at the dressing-room door and told Marvin he wanted to speak to him before he went on.

"The patrons of this establishment are exceedingly appreciative of your performance," Sparrow heard him say.

"Does that mean they like us?" Marvin asked.

"Indeed. To put it bluntly, they can't get enough of you. Would you consider extending your engagement for a further sennight?"

"What's that in English?"

"Will you stay on for another week."

"Well, that depends," Marvin replied, "on what you're offering."

"I have confidence that we can achieve a mutually satisfactory arrangement concerning remuneration."

"OK, just cut the cackle and talk turkey. How much?"

The manager winced at the American's bluntness, glanced at the other artistes moving up and down the corridor and beckoned to him.

"I would prefer not to discuss such confidential matters here," he said. "Kindly accompany me to my bureau."

"OK. I guess I've got a few minutes before we're on. Mary –" he turned back briefly to the girl as he closed the door – "I'm just going upstairs with Mr Trump. Stay put and don't talk to nobody, you hear?"

The two men had hardly turned the corner before Sparrow nipped quickly into the dressing room. Mary leapt to her feet from the sofa, excited but scared, as he rushed to open the window.

"Quick!" he told her. "Get outta your costume and

into your ordinary clothes. Go on – I won't look."

As she changed, he stuck his head out of the window and gave a low whistle. Queenie immediately appeared outside in the alley.

"It's on. Now!" Sparrow said, and threw her the velvet cloak.

Barely three minutes later, Marvin came back, passing Sparrow, who was pushing a big wicker-work basket – a skip – along the corridor. The American was so pleased with himself at being invited back for another week at the top of the bill that he even managed to give Sparrow a smile. But the smile vanished when he entered the dressing room and found Mary's scarlet costume lying on the floor, and no sign of the girl herself. He let out an angry roar, then dashed out of the room and back along the corridor, catching Sparrow just before he reached the stage door.

"Hold it right there, kid!" he cried, grabbing hold of the skip. "What you got in that basket?"

"Dirty washing, Mr Marvin, sir," Sparrow replied, his face the picture of innocence. "Ready for the Chinese laundry."

"Hah!" Marvin snarled. "You don't fool me that easy. Let's take a look, shall we?"

With a mighty heave, he turned the skip on its side, spilling its contents out onto the floor.

"Mr Marvin, sir!" Sparrow protested. "What you do that for?"

Marvin pulled at the tangled heap of sheets and clothing, baffled to find nothing more.

"Where is she?" he yelled. "What have you done with Mary?"

"Mary?" Sparrow replied. "She's in your dressing room, ain't she?"

"No, she's not, damn you! If you don't tell me—"

Alerted by Marvin's shouts, Mr Trump arrived. "If he don't tell you what?" he asked, and glared at Sparrow. "Now what have you done?"

"Me, sir? I ain't done nothin', honest. Far as I know, Miss Mary's still in her dressing room."

"And you mean she ain't, er, isn't?"

"No." Marvin shook his head and tore at his hair with his fingers. "She's gone. Disappeared! Vamoosed!"

"But … but she can't be! You're on in two minutes!" Mr Trump had gone quite pale. He shouted for Bert and, when the stage doorkeper stuck his head through the swing doors, asked him if Mary had left the theatre.

"No, sir," Bert told him. "She couldn't have come past me. Mind you, come to think of it, I did see a young lady going past outside. Wearing a red velvet cloak, she was, with the hood over her head."

"How long ago?" Mr Trump asked.

"Ooh, not more'n a couple of minutes. She went that way." He pointed to the left. Marvin charged through the doors and peered down the street. In the distance he could see a small figure in a hooded cloak just about to turn a corner.

"I see her!" he cried, and set off in hot pursuit, running as though his life depended on it.

Mr Trump turned to Sparrow.

"If you've got anything to do with this…" he threatened.

"Me, sir? No, sir. Mr Marvin told me to keep away from Miss Mary, and I been busy anyway."

Mr Trump glared at him suspiciously – but couldn't see that he was firmly crossing his fingers behind his back. Then the manager struck his forehead with the palm of his hand as he remembered the show.

"Quick," he ordered. "Run to Madame Violetta. Tell her she's to do an extra turn. I'll make the announcement."

Madame Violetta had been soothing her throat with several large glasses of gin, so she rose to the challenge happily, if a little unsteadily. As the sound of her voice warbling and wandering through a sentimental ballad floated through the theatre, Sparrow quickly made his way back to Mary's dressing room.

"It's all right," he whispered. "You can come out now."

Mary emerged from beneath the sofa, where she had been hidden by the drapes, covered in dust.

"Is it OK?" she asked. "Has he gone?"

"He's chasing Queenie all the way down Baker Street."

"Oh, my. What if he catches her?"

"He won't. She knows every twist and turn round here. And even if he did, well, he'd only find it wasn't you, right?"

"Right. That's terrific."

"Yeah, ain't it just?" Sparrow grinned triumph-antly. "Now all we gotta do is get you out of here before he finds out and comes back."

He moved quickly to open the window and help her climb out. Wiggins was waiting outside, holding an old coat of Queenie's which he wrapped around Mary's shoulders to keep her warm.

"This is Wiggins," Sparrow told her. "He's gonna take you back to HQ. You'll be safe there."

Moriarty's carriage drew up behind the Imperial Music Hall just as Marvin returned looking dis-traught. Beaver, who had stayed on to keep an eye on the place in case Sparrow needed help, watched from the dark shadow of a doorway across the street as the carriage door opened and a bony white hand beckoned the American inside. This was too good an opportunity to miss. Holding his breath, Beaver crept across to the back of the carriage, out of sight of the driver, and tried to hear the conver-sation inside it.

At first the voices were low and muffled, and he could not make out what they were saying. Then one of them, which had to be the professor's, rose in anger.

"You have let me down," he rasped. "What use are you to me if you cannot control your own step-daughter?"

"She can't have got far," Marvin replied. "She don't know London or anybody here. I'll find her."

"You'd better. Before tomorrow night."

"I will. I promise."

"Leave no stone unturned. But whatever you do, keep the police out of it."

"You don't have to tell me that."

"Just don't forget it – and don't forget tomorrow night is the big one. Now get out, and get on with it."

Beaver barely had time to scuttle back to the shadows before the door slammed behind Marvin and the carriage drove off.

"I wouldn't like to be in Marvin's shoes tomorrow," Beaver told the other Boys and Mary back at HQ, as he recounted what he had seen and heard. "The professor was furious with him."

"So was Mr Trump," Sparrow joined in. "He said

if he don't perform tomorrow night, he might as well pack his bags and go back to America, 'cos he'll make sure he never works in this country again."

"Cor," said Rosie. "Makes you feel quite sorry for him, don't it?"

"No!" Mary cried. "Never feel sorry for that man. He's wicked through and through." She burst into tears. Queenie, safely back from her mission, put her arm round her and gave her a motherly hug.

"There, there. Don't cry, love. It's all right. You're safe now."

"You don't know him like I do," Mary sobbed. "I'll never be safe as long as he's out there."

"Yeah, but you're with us now," Beaver tried to reassure her.

"That's right," Gertie joined in. "You're with the Baker Street Boys. We'll look after you. Right, everybody?"

"Right!" the others chorused.

Mary looked at their open faces and finally managed a small, slightly nervous smile.

"That's more like it," Wiggins told her. "Now, why don't we have a nice cup of cocoa, and you can tell us all about it."

"Cocoa?" she asked. "What's that?"

"It's like chocolate," said Queenie. "Only to drink. You like chocolate, don't you?"

"Oh, sure. But I'm not allowed."

"Who says?"

"Marvin. Says it'll make me fat and give me zits."

"Zits? You mean like spots? Well you ain't with Marvin no more, so you can have all the chocolate you like."

"When we can get it," Sparrow chimed in.

"Which ain't very often," Shiner added fiercely. "And when we do we have to share it."

"Of course," said Mary. "I wouldn't want more than my share of anything." And she smiled again, a little less nervously, as Queenie gave her a nod of approval.

While Queenie, with the help of Rosie and Sparrow, busied herself making cocoa with water from the big black kettle that was always singing quietly on the old stove, Wiggins sat Mary down and asked her to tell him all about Marvin.

"Like I told Sparrow," she said, "he's not my real father. My real daddy took off for the Yukon, to join the search for gold…"

"And never came back?" asked Beaver, whose own father had sailed away to the East and never returned.

"I never saw him again." Mary bit her lip, but couldn't stop a tear from rolling down her cheek. "We had word that there had been an accident in a mine that he was digging, and he'd been killed."

"Oh, that's real sad," said Gertie.

"Where's the Yukon?" Shiner asked.

"It's way over on the other side of Canada," Mary said. "Right up in the frozen north. All ice and snow and mountains and stuff. They discovered gold there."

"Did your Daddy find any?"

"I guess not. We had no money, so Ma had to look for a job. She was very beautiful, and she had a lovely voice, so Marvin took her on as his assistant. And when he promised to look after her and me, she agreed to marry him."

"Did you like that?" Rosie asked.

Mary shook her head.

"No," she said. "I always thought there was something creepy about him."

"Well, there would be, wouldn't there?" Beaver

said. "With him being a mystic and a mind-reader and all."

Mary gave a little laugh.

"Oh, that!" she said. "That's all fake. Anybody could learn it in no time."

"I knew it was!" Sparrow exclaimed. "I could see you wasn't really hypnotized."

"No, I just pretend. It's part of the act. But he can hypnotize for real."

"He can?" Rosie's eyes were wide again.

"Sure. In the other part of the act he gets people up on-stage and puts them under the 'fluence, and gets them to do all kinds of crazy things."

"What like?"

"Well, sometimes he gives them a glass of water, and tells them it's whisky or wine – and they get drunk. For real."

"On plain water?" Sparrow asked.

"Sure."

"Hey, you could make a fortune outta that," said Shiner with enthusiasm.

"Or he makes them believe they're a duck, say, or a dog," Mary continued, "and they run around the stage quacking or barking or whatever. And afterwards they don't remember anything about it, so they don't know they've been hypnotized."

"P'raps that's why you acted so funny yesterday!" Sparrow cried. "Was you hypnotized then?"

"I don't know. That's the trouble. He can make you do most anything and you just don't know."

"Anything?" Wiggins looked intrigued.

"Sure. Sometimes I wonder if that's how he got Ma to marry him."

The Boys fell silent as they thought about the enormity of this. That anyone could have such powers was scary. That the man who had them was their adversary was even more frightening.

"What happened to your ma?" Queenie asked quietly.

"She took sick and died, last year."

"So you took her place in the act," Wiggins said thoughtfully.

"I didn't want to. I hate it. But he made me."

"Of course," Wiggins said, sounding more and more like Sherlock Holmes. "What else could you do? He's the only family you've got…'

"No. No, he isn't."

"He isn't?"

"No. My ma and pa were both English. Pa was an orphan, but Ma wasn't. I guess I've got family here, maybe a grandma and grandpa and uncles and aunties too, if I could only find them."

At this, the Boys perked up. This was something they could enjoy doing.

"Don't worry," Sparrow told Mary. "We'll help you. Won't we, Wiggins?"

"We certainly will," Wiggins agreed. "But we gotta get Marvin out of the way first. No sense doing anything while he's still about."

"How we gonna do that, then?" Queenie demanded.

"I dunno just yet. But I'll think of something, trust me. First of all, we gotta find out what he's really doing with Moriarty."

Mary looked blank. "Who's Moriarty?" she asked.

"You know – the professor," Beaver explained.

"Oh, him. Now he really does give me the creeps."

"Yeah, us too," Rosie said with a shudder at the thought.

"But what's he doing with Marvin?" Wiggins repeated.

"He fixes for us to give private shows for rich

folk in their houses," Mary told him. "Makes out I'm a clairvoyant."

"Clare who?" Rosie asked.

"Clairvoyant," Gertie corrected. "That's like a fortune teller."

"How d'you know that?" Sparrow wanted to know.

"There was always one at the horse fairs my da' and me used to go to. Called herself Madame Zara, she did. Said she could tell the future."

"And could she?"

"Well, somebody set fire to her caravan once, for telling 'em wrong – she never saw that coming."

The others laughed, but Wiggins remained serious.

"Is that what you do?" he asked Mary. "Tell fortunes?"

"Sometimes. But mostly we give séances."

"Seein' what?" Shiner asked.

"Seeing nothing," Queenie explained. "A séance is like calling up spirits."

"You mean ghosts?"

"Yeah, something like that," Mary replied.

"Talking to dead people?" Gertie gasped. "Can you really do that?"

"They think so. The rich folk. They pay a deal of money to talk to their loved ones who've passed over."

"There you are, then," Beaver said. "That's what they're up to. Stinging rich people for cash."

Wiggins, however, was not convinced.

"Nah, ain't big enough, not for Moriarty," he said dismissively, then he turned back to Mary. "Do you think that's why Marvin came all the way to London?"

"I don't know. All I know is we had to leave New York in a hurry. I don't know why, but he was real jittery. Still is."

"Ha!" Wiggins exclaimed, raising one finger in the air. "The plot thickens!"

Mary looked puzzled.

"What's that mean?" she wanted to know.

"Not a lot," Queenie answered drily.

"It's what Mr Holmes says when he's getting to work on a case," Wiggins explained.

"Pity he ain't here to work on this case," Shiner moaned. "Seems to me he's never around when we need 'im."

"Mr Holmes is a very busy man," Wiggins

reproached him. "It's up to us to keep things going while he's away on other cases."

"So what we gonna do, then?" Beaver asked.

"You lot ain't gonna do nothing," Wiggins told him. "It's the middle of the night, and you're all going to get some shut-eye."

He picked up his old deerstalker hat and curly pipe from the shelf, put the hat on his head and the empty pipe in his mouth, and settled himself down in his special chair.

"I shall sit up and do some hard thinking," he said. "This is what Mr Holmes would call a three-pipe problem. I've only got one pipe, but that'll have to do."

And he clamped his teeth around the stem of the pipe and set his face in an expression of deep thoughtfulness.

Four

Next morning, as the first glimmer of light began seeping into the cellar through the grating near the ceiling, Wiggins sat upright and laid down the empty pipe that he had been sucking for most of the night.

"Got it!" he said in a satisfied voice.

Easing himself stiffly out of his chair, he stretched his arms and legs, then ambled across to the stove and poked at the coals to bring the fire back to life. The others were still asleep, curled up in their blankets in various corners. But the noise Wiggins was making with the poker soon woke them, and they got up one by one, bleary-eyed and yawning.

"Ooh, Wiggins!" protested Beaver. "What you doing that for? It's still dark."

"Yeah, I was havin' a smashing dream," Shiner grumbled. "Eatin' mutton chops and plum pudding and peppermint gobstoppers and—"

"What, all at once?" Rosie interrupted. "Yuck!"

"Oh, I dunno," said Gertie. "I wouldn't mind."

"Don't you never think of nothin' but food, Shiner?" Sparrow asked.

Shiner shook his head.

"Not when I'm 'ungry," he replied.

"You're always hungry," said Queenie, opening the larder cupboard to see if there was anything for breakfast. There were only a few stale crusts of bread and a hunk of cheese. She sighed. They had all been so busy yesterday that she had not had time to go foraging for food. She began putting the bread and cheese on the table. The others would have rushed to grab it, but she held up her hand to stop them.

"Oi!" she shouted. "Manners! Ain't you forgetting something?"

Five faces regarded her blankly, wondering what she was on about.

"We got a guest," she reminded them, nodding to Mary, who was just rising from a heap of blankets like a butterfly emerging from its chrysalis.

"Morning, Mary love, how are you?"

"I'm fine, thanks." Mary smiled at them all, still a little nervous. "I can't believe I'm really here."

"Well you are, and you're safe and sound," Beaver assured her. "Come and have some brekker."

"It ain't much, I'm afraid," said Queenie. "But help yourself all the same."

"Thanks, but I'm really not hungry," she replied.

"Can I have yours, then?" Shiner asked, quick as a flash, reaching for a piece of bread.

"No, you can't," said Queenie just as quickly, slapping his hand. "You can have your share and that's all."

"Hold on, hold on," Wiggins called out over the hubbub as everyone grabbed at the food. "Don't anybody want to know what we're gonna do?"

"Oh, yeah," said Beaver sheepishly. "Sorry, Wiggins."

"I should think so," Wiggins said. "I been up all night, you know, thinking. Now, this is what we're gonna do…"

"About finding Mary's family?" Sparrow asked eagerly.

"There's not much we can do about that just yet."

"Why not?" Queenie wanted to know. "Poor girl needs to find 'em, don't you, love?"

Mary nodded, biting her lip.

"Trouble is, you see," Wiggins explained patiently, "we don't have no clues, do we?"

"I dunno," Queenie said, turning to Mary. "Do you?"

"Only this," Mary replied, fingering the gold locket round her neck. "Marvin gave it to me — about the only kindness he ever showed me. He told me it belonged to my mother, though I don't remember seeing her wear it."

"Ain't that the one he uses to pretend to hypnotize you?" Sparrow asked.

"Yeah," she said. "He told me to keep it with me always and never let go of it. It's got a picture inside, see?"

She unlooped the chain from around her neck and pressed a little catch on the side of the locket. It opened, to reveal a tiny portrait of a lady.

"Is that your ma?" asked Queenie.

Mary shook her head. "I think it must be my grandma. But I can't be sure. My ma never talked about her family, 'cept to tell me they disowned her for marrying my daddy. And that's why she and Daddy ran away to America, before I was born."

"There you are," said Queenie. "That's a clue."

"Right," Wiggins agreed. "But first, we gotta find out what Marvin and Moriarty are up to. It's my guess that Mary won't be safe while Marvin's still on the loose."

"How are we gonna do that?" Beaver asked.

Wiggins looked around to make sure he had everyone's full attention, then spoke very slowly and carefully.

"Mary said as how the mind-reading is all a trick, right?" he began.

"Sure is," Mary said.

"And how anybody could learn how to do it in no time, right?"

"That's right. It's all to do with codes. Easy when you know how."

"So you could teach one of us – Rosie, say – how to do it?"

"Sure."

"Why me?" asked Rosie.

"Because you're near enough Mary's size, so

you could fit into her costume," Wiggins told her.

Rosie still looked bemused.

"Why would I want to do that?"

"To take her place in the act."

There was silence as the Boys tried to take in what Wiggins had said. Beaver gazed at him in admiration, but Queenie looked quite shocked.

"What?" she demanded. "You want our little Rosie to go with that terrible man?"

Rosie, though, was more scared of the audience than of Marvin.

"Me?" she gasped. "You want me to go on-stage in front of all them people?"

"Exactly."

"I couldn't."

Sparrow could hardly believe his ears. What he would have given for such a chance. If only he were a girl! But since he wasn't, he felt he had to encourage Rosie.

"Course you can," he told her. "Me and Mary will show you what to do. Won't we, Mary?"

"Sure," said Mary. "There's nothing to it. Honest. Anyways, you can't even see the audience when you've got the blindfold on. All you have to do is sit there, and remember the codes."

Reluctantly, Rosie allowed herself to be per-suaded. Wiggins's idea was for Sparrow to introduce her to Marvin and tell him that she used to work in a mind-reading act with her uncle, and knew how it was done. She could offer to stand in for Mary until Mary was found so that the show could go on. Once she was planted, Rosie would keep her eyes and ears open for any clues about what Marvin was up to, and report back to Wiggins anything she saw or heard. Mary, meanwhile, would need to lie low in HQ until it was safe for her to leave.

It was a daring and dangerous plan.

Once the scraps of bread and cheese had disap-peared, Sparrow and Mary took Rosie off into a corner to start rehearsing her role. Between them, they described the act to her and told her what she would have to do, warning her about the pin and the blindfold and the fake hypnosis. Luckily, she was a quick learner and soon got the hang of it. But it was harder when they came to the codes.

"See, what happens is," Mary explained, "Marvin goes down into the audience and asks people to give him stuff. People always have the same sorts of things in their pockets or their purses, so there's not all that much to learn. You just have to listen carefully to what he says. If he says 'Right, Mary...' then you know it's a pen that he's holding."

"How do I know?"

"Because that's what a pen does: it writes. OK?"

Rosie still looked puzzled, but Sparrow's face lit up as he twigged.

"Oh, I got you!" he said. "Right, write – it ain't the same but it sounds the same."

"That's it. You see, Rosie?"

"Yeah, I think so," Rosie answered, a bit worried about how much she would have to remember.

"And if he says 'Take your *time*', or even 'This *time*...', then you know it's a watch. You get a lot of watches – every gentleman has one in his pocket."

"Ooh, that's an easy one," said Sparrow, who was starting to enjoy this. "Give us some more."

"OK. If he says 'around' – like 'I have my hand around an object' – then it's a ring."

"'Cos a ring's round!" Sparrow chirped excitedly.

"Sparrow," Rosie chided. "I'm the one what's supposed to be learning all this!"

"Oh, yeah. Sorry," he said sheepishly. "Got a bit carried away."

Mary smiled at him, pleased by his enthusiasm. He blushed, and she continued listing all the code words. "Stick at it" or "stick with it" meant a brooch, because of brooches having pins at the back to stick into dresses or jackets; "wipe", as in "wipe everything from your mind", meant a handkerchief; "hold on" meant a wallet or pocket-book, since a wallet holds money; a snuff box was indicated by the phrase "who knows?" – "knows" signifying "nose"; a cigarette-case was signalled by a cough followed by "pardon me"; and so it went on.

Rosie's head was spinning as she tried to remember everything, but they went on practising all through the morning, and by early afternoon Mary and Sparrow pronounced her ready for a trial performance in front of the Boys. Wiggins had a watch, but they had no brooches or cigarette cases, or coins like sovereigns or half-crowns, or indeed most of the things that audiences regularly lent to Marvin. So Mary wrote the names of the objects on scraps of paper, which she gave to the other Boys. Then, when Rosie was "hypnotized", Mary moved among them, took the pieces of paper, one by one, and called out the code words. To the delight – and amazement – of the Boys, Rosie responded with the right answer every time. It was a triumph. The only question was, could she do it for Marvin, and in front of an audience?

It was teatime before Sparrow and Rosie arrived at the theatre, and wisps of fog were starting to swirl around the streets and alleys. Old Ant, the baked potato man, had set up his barrow near by, and the smell of the hot potatoes and the warmth of the oven were very tempting as they passed. But Wiggins, who was walking just behind them with Beaver, told them there was no time to linger, and hurried them along.

"You're early, young 'un," Bert greeted Sparrow as he passed through the stage door. "There's hours to go afore the show."

"I know," Sparrow replied. "I gotta see Mr Trump. And Mr Marvin."

"Well, you're in luck. They're both in the office. Mind, you'll have to tread very careful," he warned. "The guv'nor ain't in the best of tempers, and you know what he's like when he's roused."

"Yeah, but I might be able to cheer him up."

"Found Miss Mary, have you?"

"Next best thing," Sparrow told him, jauntily. "Come on, Rosie. This way."

Rosie had never been backstage, and Sparrow had to whisper to her not to stare at everything but to try and look as though she had seen it all before. She did her best, but still gazed wide-eyed around her as he led her behind the scenery and up the staircase to the manager's office. The sound of angry voices from inside the room made her even more nervous, and Sparrow squeezed her hand tightly as he knocked on the door.

"What do you want?" Mr Trump barked at Sparrow when he poked his head round the door. "Can't you see I'm busy? I've got no star turn for tonight's show!"

"That's what I've come about," Sparrow replied, noticing that in the manager's agitation he had quite forgotten his usual flowery phrases and was speaking plain English.

"Oh, yes?" Mr Trump said with heavy sarcasm. "Offering to go on instead of Marvin, are you?

Fancy yourself topping the bill?"

"No, sir. I mean, yes I do, but not just yet."

Mr Trump turned to look at Marvin, who was slumped in a chair looking fraught and dejected, and jerked a thumb at Sparrow.

"What do you think of your replacement, then?" he sneered.

"I got no time for jokes," Marvin snapped. "Get him outta here."

"You heard the man," Mr Trump said. "Hop it!"

"No, wait," said Sparrow.

He opened the door wider and pulled Rosie into view. Queenie had raided the clothes chest in HQ and had dressed Rosie up in a long skirt and a frilly blouse, with a lacy shawl round her shoulders and a battered straw hat on her head, all much too big for her and all in bright, clashing colours. She had done her best to brush her hair, but Rosie's fair curls still fell in a tangle around her face. Mr Trump stared open-mouthed at this apparition.

"This is Rosie," Sparrow announced.

"So what," said Marvin. "We don't have time for this…"

"Ah, time!" Sparrow interrupted, raising a lordly

hand. "Now then, Rosie, take your time. What is this object I am holding up?"

"It is … it is a watch," Rosie replied.

Marvin sat up, suddenly alert. Sparrow continued in his best showman style.

"Very good, my dear," he said. "Now, what is this in my right hand?"

"It's a gold coin," Rosie answered, remembering that "right hand" meant gold and "left hand" meant silver.

"What sort of a gold coin? Think carefully, now. Think very carefully."

Rosie put her fingers to her forehead, pretending to be concentrating. In the code, one "think" meant a half-sovereign, two "thinks" a sovereign.

"It is a sovereign," she declared confidently. "A gold sovereign."

Marvin was on his feet now.

"Where did you learn that?" he asked.

"I used to do a mind-reading act with my uncle," Rosie told him.

"Where?"

"Up north," Sparrow chipped in hurriedly. "Right up north."

"So why did you stop?" Marvin looked at her suspiciously.

Rosie bit her lip as she tried to think of what to say. This was not something they had thought of.

"I, er ... I ran away," she said finally. "He was very cruel."

Sparrow kicked her ankle to stop her going any further.

"And he drank, didn't he?" he said quickly. "Drank something terrible."

"Oh, er, yeah. Yeah. Like a fish."

"Well, that's as may be," Mr Trump said, beginning to look and sound more like his usual self. "But your relative's misfortune is exceedingly serendipitous in relation to our good selves."

"Eh?" Rosie looked at him blankly. He sighed.

"Bad luck for your uncle, good luck for us," he translated.

"Oh, right. Why didn't you say so?"

"I did."

"Never mind all that," Marvin butted in. "Can you remember the codes?"

"Course she can," Sparrow said. "Go on – ask her anything you like."

"Oh, I will," said Marvin. He circled Rosie, inspecting her carefully.

"Well?" Mr Trump asked him. "Does she appear to be satisfactory?"

Marvin took off Rosie's hat, and fingered her tangled hair. Then he nodded.

"She'll do," he said. "Till Mary shows up again."

"Have you given consideration to her apparel?" asked Mr Trump. "She can't go on like that."

"She can wear Mary's costume. She's not that much smaller."

"That's what I thought," said Sparrow.

"Did you indeed? You appear to have thought of everything," said Mr Trump. "Enlighten me – how did you locate this fair maiden?"

"Oh, er, she's my cousin, sort of. Ain't you, Rosie?"

Rosie nodded nervously, but before the manager could ask any more awkward questions, Marvin cut the conversation short.

"C'mon, kid," he said. "We gotta lot of work to do, and no time to do it in." And he led her away to start rehearsing.

Mr Trump watched them go, then turned back to

Sparrow with a mistrustful expression on his face.

"I have a powerful presentiment," he pronounced, "that you are up to something. It is immaterial to me, as long as I have a show tonight. But I warn you, my lad, if anything should go amiss, you'll be for it in a big way."

FIVE

Rosie sat on Mary's little gold chair in the centre of
the stage, staring out at the rows and rows of empty
seats in the theatre. She could not help but imagine them as they would be that evening, filled with
people, all with their eyes on her. It was a terrifying
thought. Her mind froze. Marvin's voice sounded
far away, as though he was speaking to her from the
other end of a very long tunnel.

"Rosie? Rosie!"

When she did not respond, he took hold of her
shoulders and shook her.

"What's up, kid?" he demanded. "You scared or
something?"

Watching from a dark corner in the wings,
Sparrow bit his fingernails anxiously. Stage fright
– it was something he had not counted on. If Rosie

was stricken with stage fright the whole plan would collapse. He willed her to be brave.

"I … I'm always nervous before a show," he heard her say.

To his surprise, Marvin did not seem to be angry.

"OK, kid," he said. "Take it easy now. I can fix that – after all, we don't want you getting nerves and forgetting your codes, do we?"

Rosie shook her head.

"I can stop you feeling scared."

"How?"

"By hypnotizing you."

"Oh, no," Sparrow muttered. What if Rosie let out the truth once she was hypnotized?

"All you have to do is relax, and leave everything to me," Marvin told Rosie. "Trust me, I can make you remember things."

And forget things, Sparrow thought.

He watched helplessly as the American put Rosie into a trance and told her that she would not be scared of facing the audience: they were all her friends. He added that she had nothing to worry about. If she seemed to be forgetting the codes or getting too nervous, he would put her under hypnosis again very simply.

"All I have to do," he said, "is say the magic words and snap my fingers, like this." He demonstrated with a loud click. "Do you understand?"

"I understand," Rosie answered in a flat voice.

"Excellent. The magic words are 'hocus pocus'. Hocus pocus," he repeated. "Have you got that?"

"The magic words are hocus pocus," Rosie replied.

"Good. Now, I shall count down from five to zero, and when I click my fingers again, you will wake up."

Outside the theatre, Wiggins and Beaver were huddled in a doorway near the baked potato barrow, trying to keep warm by the heat of the coke fire under the portable oven. They had managed to wheedle a couple of hot potatoes and a lump of salt out of Old Ant earlier, but they were still feeling the chill of the raw day and could hardly wait to get back to HQ. While there was still no news from inside the theatre, though, they had to stay put and wait for Sparrow to report. And while they were waiting, they couldn't help but notice that they were not the only ones keeping an eye on the stage door.

Wiggins strolled casually over to the baked potato man and spoke quietly to him.

"'Ere, Ant," he said, "don't look now, but there's a geezer been stood across the road there all afternoon. He's been trying to keep out of sight in the shadows, but I clocked him straight off."

"So what?" said Old Ant. Nobody knew why he was called that – maybe his real name was Anthony – but it suited him perfectly, for he was a thin little man who looked like an overgrown insect with his bent back, large head and wizened face. "It's a free country, ain't it? He can stand where he likes if he ain't doin' no harm to nobody."

"Fair enough," Wiggins agreed. "But have you ever seen him afore?"

Old Ant cast a swift glance across the street, then shook his head.

"Can't say as I 'ave."

"No, nor me neither."

Before Wiggins could think any more about the mystery man in the shadows, the stage door opened and Sparrow came out, beckoning to his two friends.

"He bought it," he told them. "Rosie's goin' on tonight."

Wiggins's face broke into a broad smile. Quickly Sparrow sketched in what had happened in the music hall and assured him that Rosie was going to be all right.

"You done good," Wiggins praised him. "Now, you'd best get back inside and keep an eye on her. Beaver and me'll leg it back to HQ and let the others know."

Slapping Sparrow on the back and giving a quick wave to Old Ant, Wiggins bustled off down the street, with Beaver loping alongside him. They had not gone far before Beaver spoke.

"Wiggins," he said, "that geezer's following us."

"You could be right," Wiggins replied. "Best make sure, though, eh?"

They turned sharply into a side street and kept walking. Sure enough, a few moments later the man turned the corner too, a dark figure in a black overcoat with a cape on the shoulders, moving through the gloom with a heavy limp. As he passed into the pool of light cast by a street lamp, they could see that he had a black beard and deep-set eyes. Another corner, another turning, and still he appeared behind them. There could be no doubt about it: he was on their trail.

"Right," Wiggins muttered to Beaver out of the side of his mouth. "You know what to do."

"Yeah," Beaver replied. "Let's lose him."

They sped up and split up, going different ways at the next turning, each cutting through alleyways and courts, doubling back on themselves and even nipping through buildings to make sure the man could have no idea where they had gone. Eventually, by the most roundabout route, they both arrived back at HQ, within a minute of each other, confident that they had given their pursuer the slip.

The other Boys and Mary were waiting anxiously for news of Rosie, and were relieved to hear that everything seemed to be going well. They all wanted to go to the theatre that night to watch the performance, but Wiggins said that was too risky. If Mr Trump saw them all together, he might start asking why they were there and suspect that they were friends of Rosie's.

"Anyway," he went on, "we can't leave Mary on her own. So me and Beaver will go back and keep an eye on things at the theatre, and the rest of you stop here."

Shiner grumbled at this, but Queenie said she could see the sense in it and told him to shut up. He obeyed her by going into one of his sulks, but Mary got him out of it by saying she would feel much safer with him there as well as Queenie and Gertie.

"That's right," Wiggins said. "I reckon there's some bloke out there looking for her. He ain't a copper, that's for sure. He's likely working for Marvin. Or even Moriarty."

At the mention of Moriarty, the others caught their breath. Wiggins told them about the mystery man who had tried to follow him and Beaver. He described him to Mary, and asked her if she knew anyone like that. She shook her head.

"Never mind," he said. "Just remember, whoever he is, he's out there. So we've all gotta be on our guard, right?"

Waiting until the show had started and the first few acts had finished, Wiggins and Beaver managed to sneak in through the side door of the theatre and up the stairs to the gallery. Right up under the roof, the gallery – usually called "the gods" – was the cheapest part of the theatre, and for good reason. It was hot, smoky and noisy, and not very comfortable. There were no individual seats, just hard, narrow benches curving across the width of the auditorium. And it was so steep that the two Boys felt quite giddy looking down at the stage and the tops of the performers' heads.

The people sitting on the top row shuffled along to make room for the Boys, and they soon felt part of the happy crowd. On-stage, a pretty young woman was singing a popular song, and Wiggins couldn't help grinning as he heard the words:

"The boy I love is up in the gallery,
The boy I love is looking down at me,
There he is, can't you see, a waving of his
*   handkerchief,*
As merry as a robin that sings on a tree..."

All the young men around Wiggins and Beaver took out their handkerchiefs and waved them like mad, and everybody laughed.

As the different acts followed each other for the rest of the evening, all of them highly entertaining,

Wiggins had to keep reminding himself that he was there on serious business. Beaver, too, was quite carried away by it all. He could see, he whispered to Wiggins, why Sparrow loved the music hall so much.

"Me and all," Wiggins answered, then added in a low voice, "but we ain't here to enjoy ourselves, Beav. We gotta keep our eyes open and our minds on the job."

"Right," Beaver agreed. But he couldn't take his eyes off the stage as Signor Macarelli's knives whistled through the air and thudded into the board around his wife. If one of those knives should miss its mark... Beaver held his breath and shuddered at the thought.

Behind the scenes, Rosie was getting more and more nervous as she waited to go on. Marvin kept her in the dressing room rehearsing right up to the very last minute, so Sparrow had no chance to speak to her or even to see her until she stood in the wings ready to go on. Dressed in Mary's costume, with her face made up and her hair tied back with ribbons, she looked very like Mary – so like her that

Sparrow was sure no one in the audience would know the difference. Which was just what Marvin and Mr Trump wanted.

"Good luck, girl," Sparrow told her. "Knock 'em cold."

Rosie did not reply. She stared straight ahead, as though she did not even know he was there. Before Sparrow could say any more, Marvin had taken Rosie's hand and led her on to the stage, to the sound of loud applause.

With Sparrow watching anxiously from the wings and Wiggins and Beaver peering down from the gods, Marvin began the act. Because Rosie did not have Mary's locket round her neck, he could not use it to "hypnotize" her, so he made do with his pocket watch on its gold chain. But everything else was the same. Marvin even called her "Mary" so no one would know they were not watching the real thing. Soon he was moving among the audience and borrowing things for Rosie, now blindfolded, to identify. Just as Mary had said, the objects people handed him were the same as usual: pens, watches, purses, coins, cigarette cases – all the things for which she had learned the codes.

Everything was going perfectly smoothly until a man handed Marvin a small piece of paper. Marvin looked at it, then stopped short. The colour drained from his face. He staggered, as though about to faint, then stuffed the note into his pocket and continued with the next object as though nothing had happened. Because Marvin was underneath the balcony, Wiggins and Beaver could not see what was going on. Nor could Rosie, from behind her blindfold. But Sparrow, who was peeping round the scenery, saw the mind-reader move quickly away from the man and head back to the stage. He watched curiously as Marvin finished the act in a hurry, took his bow with Rosie, then hustled her away and back to the dressing room.

"Was I all right?" Rosie asked as Marvin closed the door behind her and turned the key in the lock. His face was tense and pale.

"Never mind about that," he snapped. "We gotta get outta here. Fast."

To Rosie's bewilderment he began grabbing his belongings and shoving them into a bag as though his life depended on it. There was a loud knock at the door. Rosie was about to open it, but Marvin grabbed her by the arm, dragged her across the room and started opening the window.

"Leave it!" he hissed. "C'mon – we'll leave this way."

In the dressing-room corridor, Mr Trump knocked on the door again. Getting no reply, he tried the door, then shrugged and walked away. At the end of the corridor he met Sparrow and asked him if he had seen Marvin since he came off-stage.

"Yes, sir," Sparrow told him. "He went straight to his dressing room. Looked like he was in a real hurry."

"Are you sure? He doesn't appear to be there now."

"He's gotta be."

"Hmm." Mr Trump thought for a moment. "He must have departed for one of his private engagements. Pity. I wished to congratulate him – and, of course, your, er, cousin. Perhaps you will tell her when you see her?"

"Right, sir. I will."

Mr Trump went on his way, humming happily to himself. But Sparrow was not happy. Sensing that something was wrong, he ran down the corridor and banged on Marvin's door.

"Mr Marvin!" he called out. And when there was no reply, "Rosie! Rosie, are you there?"

He was sure he heard a sound from inside the room, but no one answered. He turned the knob and pushed, but the door would not open. Bending down, he tried to peer through the keyhole but could see nothing. Something seemed to be blocking it. Then he realized what it was: the key was in the lock – on the inside of the door. He stood for a moment, wondering what to do, then turned and charged down the corridor and out of the stage door, past a startled Bert.

"Oi! Oi!" the doorkeeper yelled after him. "Where's the fire?"

But Sparrow didn't stop. Outside, he looked around frantically for Wiggins and Beaver. He finally saw them strolling round the corner from the front of the theatre, and dashed breathlessly to them.

"Quick! Quick!" he gasped. "This way!"

"Whoa, whoa!" Wiggins said. "Hold your horses, Sparrow."

"What's up?" Beaver asked. "Rosie did good, didn't she?"

"Yeah, but somethin's wrong," Sparrow blurted out, and quickly told them about the locked door and getting no response from inside the dressing room.

"The window," said Wiggins, leading the way down the alley behind the dressing rooms. "We can see in through the window. Now, which one is it?"

"That one," Sparrow said, and pointed. "The one what's wide open."

They hurried to the window and looked in. Inside the room a dark figure in a heavy overcoat was crouched over a bundle of something on the floor. Wiggins let out a shout, and the man looked up. It was the bearded man who had tried to follow them in the street.

"It's him!" Wiggins cried. "Get him!"

He started to clamber through the window. The man stared at them for a brief moment, then straightened up and rushed to the door. He swiftly unlocked it, dashed through and down the corridor and escaped into the street, past a startled Bert. The Boys tried to give chase, but he had too much of a head start and by the time they got to the stage door he had disappeared into the night. Bert came out behind them, scratching his head.

"'Ere! What's goin' on?" he asked. "Where did you come from? Who was that? What's he doin' here?"

"That's what we want to know," Wiggins said.

"What was he doin' in the dressin' room?" Beaver asked.

"Dunno," Wiggins replied. "Let's go and see."

Followed by a protesting Bert, Wiggins led the way back to the dressing room. The door was wide open and the "bundle" that the man had been crouching over was still on the floor – only now they could see that it was not a bundle but a body, lying face down. It was the body of Marvin. And he was dead. Very dead, with a large knife sticking out of his back.

SIX

"Stabbed," Inspector Lestrade announced, looking down at the body. "From behind. Right through the heart."

Mr Trump, who was standing in the doorway of the dressing room, sighed heavily.

"This is dreadful," he said. "Truly dreadful…'

"Yes, indeed," Lestrade agreed. "If it's any comfort, I can tell you he would have died instantly."

But it was not Marvin's fate that was upsetting Mr Trump.

"I've lost my star turn," he moaned. "What am I going to do?"

"You are going to assist me with my inquiries."

Mr Trump looked shocked.

"Inspector!" he exclaimed. "You surely don't imagine that I know anything about this terrible crime?"

"No, sir. But it took place in your theatre and there's things I need to know that I'm sure you can tell me."

"Ah, I see," said Mr Trump, greatly relieved not to be a suspect. "In that case, I shall be gratified to avail you of the benefit of my cognizance."

Lestrade blinked at him, wondering what on earth he was on about.

"I'll be happy to tell you everything I know," Mr Trump translated.

"Right," said Lestrade. "Who found the body?"

"We did," Wiggins called out from the corridor.

He stepped forward, followed by Beaver and Sparrow. Bert, determined not to be left out, pushed his way in behind them.

"And me," he said.

Lestrade stared at the Boys in disbelief.

"Oh, no," he groaned. "Not you lot. Please don't tell me Mr Holmes is mixed up in this."

"No, he ain't. He's miles away on another case."

"We must be grateful for small mercies, I suppose," Lestrade sighed.

"But Professor Moriarty is," Beaver told him.

Lestrade groaned again. "I suppose you've seen him, have you?"

"I did," Sparrow said. "Sittin' outside this very theatre, he was, in his carriage."

"Tonight?"

"No. Two nights ago."

"I see." Lestrade clearly did not believe him.

"And Marvin went off with him after the show," Sparrow went on. "I seen 'em go."

"I don't suppose you know where they went?" Lestrade asked in a sarcastic voice. "Or what they were going to do?"

"They was goin' to give a private see … seeing…"

"Séance," Wiggins said.

"Yeah," Sparrow continued. "One of them. In a posh house somewhere."

"How do you know that?"

"Mary told me."

"Mary?"

"Little Mary," Mr Trump explained. "Mr Marvin's assistant. "She absconded last night."

The inspector raised his eyebrows and pushed back his bowler hat.

"Did she indeed?" he said. "Little Mary runs

away last night, and tonight Mr Marvin is murdered. Sounds to me like there could well be a connection."

"No, there ain't," Sparrow piped up. "Mary didn't have nothin' to do with it. She couldn't have."

"How do you know that?"

"Because she's – ow!" he cried as Wiggins kicked him fiercely on the ankle. "I just do. She's not that sort of girl."

"I see. When did she tell you about this séance? Before she ran away?"

Sparrow hesitated, and just stopped himself in time. He nodded.

"Never mind Mary," Beaver piped up. "What about Rosie? What's happened to her?"

Lestrade held up his hand to calm him.

"All in good time," he said, and turned back to Wiggins. "First things first. Tell me how you came to find the body."

Wiggins quickly explained, taking care not to say anything about Mary or their part in her escape. When he described the bearded man, Lestrade looked doubtful.

"Are you quite certain of this, Wiggins?" he asked. "How could you have seen him so clearly in such a short space of time?"

"We seen him afore," Wiggins replied. "We seen him yesterday outside the theatre. He tried to trail us, but we gave him the slip."

"That's right," Beaver confirmed. "You can ask Old Ant the 'tater man. He seen him and all."

"And I seen him tonight," Bert chipped in. "I seen him racing past my box after he done it."

"Ah," said Lestrade. "Corroboration at last."

"Eh?" asked Bert.

"Backing up what they say," Mr Trump explained helpfully.

"So," Lestrade said to Wiggins, "you clearly saw the murderer but you did not see the actual crime?"

"No, sir, more's the pity. If we'd been a minute earlier, we might have been able to stop it."

"Or got stabbed yourselves," Mr Trump said lugubriously.

"Never mind," Lestrade continued. "We shall find him, have no fear."

"You gotta find Rosie first," Wiggins reminded him.

"Wiggins is right," Beaver said. "Where is she?"

"Who is this Rosie?"

"Mr Marvin's temporary assistant, in the absence of Little Mary," Mr Trump told him.

"You mean like an understudy?" Lestrade asked.

"In a manner of speaking, yes."

"Look," said Wiggins urgently. "You gotta find her. She was in here when Marvin was topped. What's happened to her?"

"In here, was she? With him?"

"That's correct," Mr Trump said. "I can vouch for the verisimilitude of that."

"She could be in terrible danger!" Beaver cried. "We gotta find her. Quick."

He turned to go, but Lestrade signalled to a large police constable standing in the corridor, who blocked his way.

"Nobody leaves this theatre, my lad, until I say so," Lestrade told him. "This Rosie has obviously run away because she was in league with the murderer. She probably let him in through the window. Unless it was somebody else already in the building."

He leaned over the body and pulled the knife out of Marvin's back. It was a long stiletto with a sharply pointed blade dripping with blood. He held it up under the nose of Mr Trump, who gulped and turned quite pale.

"I understand that one of your acts is a knife-thrower," the inspector said with great seriousness.

Sparrow was sent to fetch Signor Macarelli, who arrived on the scene looking very agitated, loudly protesting his innocence and his ignorance of anything that had happened. His wife followed him down the corridor, weeping and wailing even more loudly. Lestrade glared at them.

"Now then, Mr Macaroni," he began.

"Macarelli," the knife-thrower corrected him. "Is-a Macarelli. I notta pasta."

"Never mind all that," Lestrade continued, speaking very slowly and loudly and separating each word, although Signor Macarelli understood English perfectly well. "Do … you … know … anything … about … this?"

He pointed to Marvin's body, then held up the knife. Signor Macarelli examined it with professional interest, then shook his head. His wife let out a howl behind him.

"Is-a no' mine," he said. "Is-a trash made in America, not Italia. No good for throw, only for stabbing."

And he demonstrated by miming a stabbing so realistically that the Boys and Mr Trump all shuddered with horror. Signora Macarelli howled again, louder than ever.

"Well, it's good for that, right enough," Lestrade replied. "Very well, Signor, you … can … go … back … to … your … room … for … now."

"And take your wife with you," added Mr Trump. "Please!"

As Signora Macarelli's sobs and moans died away down the corridor, Lestrade moved around the dressing room, looking for clues. The three Boys watched him closely, in case they spotted anything he might have missed.

"It would appear," said the inspector, opening the bag into which Marvin had been stuffing his clothes and belongings, "that our mind-reader was intending to make a hurried departure but was interrupted by his murderer. Interesting… Now, what have we here?"

He opened a long wardrobe and looked at the clothes hanging inside.

"Rosie's clothes!" Sparrow exclaimed.

"That means wherever she's gone, she's still

wearing her stage costume," Wiggins declared.

"Mary's stage costume," Sparrow corrected him.

"Why didn't she get changed?" Beaver worried. "She'll catch her death of cold out there."

"Quiet!" shouted Lestrade. "I'm the one who asks the questions here!"

"Sorry, Inspector," said Wiggins courteously. "Do go on. Please."

Lestrade gave him a hard stare – he had sounded uncomfortably like Sherlock Holmes letting the inspector make a fool of himself.

"Clearly," he said, "the girl was in too much of a hurry making her escape. But she'll discover she cannot escape from Scotland Yard. We shall find her. We shall find them both – Rosie and Mary. I shall start a manhunt."

"Don't you mean girl-hunt?" Wiggins asked innocently.

"And your bearded villain," Lestrade went on, ignoring the interruption. "I shall circulate their details to every member of the Metropolitan Police Force. We shall cast a net over the whole of London."

He looked around the room again and nodded.

"Nothing more to do here, apart from removing the body," he said. "So you lot can go home."

He waved the Boys to the door, but as they turned, Sparrow caught sight of a small square of paper on the floor near Marvin's body. He bent down to pick it up.

"Look, Inspector," he called out. "What's this?"

Lestrade glanced at the paper.

"A note?" he asked. "Anything written on it?"

"No," Sparrow told him. "There ain't nothin' on it, 'cepting a bit of blood."

"Which is not surprising," Lestrade replied, handing it back to him. "Obviously of no importance."

Sparrow was not so sure. He wondered if it might be the piece of paper that had been handed to Marvin in the audience that had given him such a shock. He tried to tell the inspector this, but Lestrade cut him short and sent him on his way. Sparrow shrugged, slipped the paper into his pocket and followed Wiggins and Beaver out.

"What we gonna do about Rosie, then?" Beaver asked when they got outside the stage door. "What d'you think's happened to her?"

"Probably took fright and scarpered," Wiggins said. "I know if I'd seen somethin' like that, I'd have got out fast as I could and run all the way home. I reckon that's where she'll be – safe and sound at HQ."

But Rosie was not safe and sound at HQ. When the three Boys arrived back, they found no sign of her. At first the others could not understand why Wiggins, Beaver and Sparrow were so worried.

"Rosie'll be all right," said Gertie. "Sure and doesn't she know the streets round here as well as anyone."

"I dare say she's lyin' low somewhere," Queenie said. "She's a sensible girl, after all."

"Course she is," Shiner agreed, then asked eagerly, "Was there a lot of blood?"

"Not as much as you might think," Beaver told him. "Course, it could have all been underneath the body..."

"Oh, please, don't," Mary begged, bursting into tears. "I can't stand it."

"Sorry," Beaver apologized. "I oughta have thought – him bein' your stepdad and all..."

Queenie put her arms around Mary and gave her a hug. But it didn't seem to comfort her.

"It's all my fault," she cried. "I better give myself up to the police."

"Don't talk so daft," Wiggins said. "What good's that gonna do anybody?"

"I know I hated him, but I never wanted him murdered. I could tell them that."

"They wouldn't listen to you. Not Inspector Lestrade. All he'd do is lock you up in a orphanage, and you wouldn't want that, would you?"

Mary shook her head.

"An orphanage … gee, I guess it would be. If I can't find my ma's family, I got nobody now…"

"Just like the rest of us, love," said Queenie cheerfully. "So you'd best stick with us."

"Anyway," Wiggins continued, "if you did go to the police, you'd only be getting us into trouble."

"How come?"

"They'd say we lured you away from the theatre. Might even think we had something to do with the murder."

"Oh, no!" Mary looked quite shocked. "They couldn't!"

"You don't know old Lestrade like I do. No, best thing you can do is stop 'ere with us till Mr Holmes and Dr Watson gets back. If anybody can find your family it's Mr Holmes."

"You really think he could?"

"Course. Mr Holmes can do anything."

"And if he can't," Sparrow assured her, "we will."

Mary managed a weak smile, and Queenie gave her another hug.

"Come on," she said, "it'll be morning afore we knows where we are. Time we all got some shut-eye."

Reminded of how late it was, and how tired they were, most of the Boys began yawning and rubbing their eyes.

"What about Rosie?" Beaver asked. "I think I'll go and look for her."

"In the dark?" Queenie said. "It's pitch black out there."

"Queenie's right," said Wiggins. "You'll never see a thing. Best wait till morning."

"She'll be back by then, anyway," Gertie said. "Just you wait and see."

The others nodded sleepily, and headed for their beds. But Beaver was still worrying.

"It ain't like her to stop out," he muttered as he pulled his blanket round his head.

Despite his fears, he was so weary that he fell asleep at once. But he dreamed of Rosie being chased along dark streets and alleyways by a bearded man with a limp, brandishing a large knife dripping with blood.

SEVEN

When the Boys woke the next morning, there was
still no sign of Rosie. Beaver would have set out to
search for her right away, but Wiggins said they
had to plan what they were going to do, and where
they were going to go. And Queenie insisted that
they all have some breakfast first, even though it
was only crusts again.

As he sat down and chewed on the stale bread,
Sparrow dipped his hand into the pocket of his coat
and pulled out the piece of paper he had picked up
from the dressing-room floor. He smoothed it out
and stared at it, trying to make sense of it.

"What you got there?" Shiner asked, and
snatched it away.

"You give that back!" Sparrow yelled, trying to
grab it. "I found it. It's a clue!"

"Garn!" scoffed Shiner. "It's only a bit of paper. What's this on it?"

"Blood."

"Marvin's blood? Crikey…"

"No, it ain't Marvin's."

"Whose is it then – the murderer's?

"P'raps."

The others fell silent as they heard this, staring with awe at the small square of paper. Wiggins picked it up and examined it carefully.

"Yeah, I reckon it's blood right enough," he said. "Where'd you get it?"

Sparrow told him about finding it next to the body, and how Lestrade had dismissed it as being unimportant.

"Why ain't it Marvin's blood, then?" Beaver asked.

"'Cos it was old," Sparrow told him. "And dry. If it had been Marvin's from the stabbin', it'd have been fresh and sticky."

"Good thinking," Wiggins congratulated him. "We'll make a detective out of you yet."

"But that ain't all," Sparrow said, and proceeded to tell them about the man in the audience passing something to Marvin, and how Marvin had reacted.

"He was real scared," he said. "He tried to hide it, but I could see."

"Why didn't you tell Lestrade about this?" Wiggins asked.

"I tried to, but he wouldn't listen."

Wiggins nodded thoughtfully, stroked his chin and studied the piece of paper again. The others watched him, waiting for words of wisdom.

"This ain't no *splash* of blood," he announced at last. "This has been done very careful. Look, it's somebody's thumb. Somebody's pricked their thumb, or dipped it in blood, and pressed it down to make a mark right in the middle of the paper."

"I know what it is!" Queenie exclaimed. "It's the black spot!"

"Don't be daft," Shiner jeered. "Anybody can see that ain't black."

"Don't matter," said Queenie. "It's the same thing."

She told them about one of the books she used to read to her mother when she was really ill, a marvellous story called *Treasure Island*. It was all about pirates, she said, and when they'd tracked down one of them who'd cheated the others and stolen the treasure map, they gave him a piece of paper with a black spot in the middle of it, as a warning that if he didn't give it back they would kill him.

"You mean Marvin was really a pirate?" Gertie asked. "Oh, my!"

"Of course he weren't a pirate," Wiggins told her. "Ain't no such thing no more."

"But he could have been a crook," said Queenie. "He could have cheated on his mates and they could have been out to get him."

"What d'you think, Mary?" Wiggins asked.

Mary thought hard for a moment, then said, "Yeah, could be. Maybe that's why we had to leave America in such a hurry."

"That's it, then," said Wiggins. "Marvin belonged to some secret society, like the Black Hand Gang, and he done the dirty on 'em. So they'd want their revenge. And this – " he held up the piece of paper – "was to let him know they'd caught up with him. That they were gonna kill him."

The others stared in horror at the bloodstained paper. Then Queenie let out an anguished cry: "Rosie!"

The Boys began to panic at the thought of the danger Rosie was in, but Wiggins held up his hand and called for calm. There were two things that could have happened, he reasoned. The murderer could have taken Rosie, to keep her quiet. Or she could have escaped and was hiding somewhere, too scared to come out in case the murderer caught her.

"If she is hiding," Wiggins said, "we gotta find her before the murderer does, and bring her back here."

"Yeah, but what if he's got her locked up somewhere? What do we do then?" Beaver asked.

"Keep our eyes peeled and our ears open for any clues to where she might be," Wiggins answered. And ask everybody we know if they've seen the geezer with the black beard and the limp."

Leaving Queenie to look after Mary, the remaining Boys set off on their hunt. Wiggins and Shiner went off in one direction, while Beaver and Gertie went the other way. They were soon poking into every corner and searching every nook and cranny, every back court and alleyway around Baker Street, calling Rosie's name and questioning everybody they met. But it was soon obvious that the little flower girl was nowhere to be found.

Sparrow headed back to the theatre, to see if he could spot any clues that might have been missed the night before. The stage door was shut, so he crept round the side of the building and down the alley behind the dressing rooms. The window of Marvin's room was closed, but Sparrow knew the catches on all the windows were old and worn, and he soon managed to undo it with his penknife. Glancing back to make sure nobody was watching, he climbed inside, carefully sliding the window shut behind him.

To his great relief, Marvin's body had been taken away, though a large bloodstain showed where it had lain. He tiptoed carefully past this, and began looking around. But he had not got very far when he heard the sounds of someone in the corridor, and a key being inserted into the lock. His heart almost stopped beating as he saw the doorknob turning. There was no time to get back through the window. Instead, he yanked open the door to the wardrobe, dived inside and pulled it shut. Hiding behind Rosie's clothes, he heard someone enter the room.

"This here's his dressing room, madam," came the familiar voice of Bert. "But I can't let you go in."

"Oh, please," an American woman's voice pleaded. "It's real important to me … would this help?"

Sparrow heard the chink of coins, then Bert spoke again.

"Well, I don't know. I got my job to think about …'

"It means so much to me," the woman said. "It was a gift from my dear departed husband. It would break my heart to lose it."

There was more chinking of coins.

"Well, just for a minute, mind," said Bert.

"You are a dear, sweet man. Thank you so much."

Sparrow huddled into the corner of the cupboard, hardly daring to breathe, listening to the sounds of the woman moving around the room. Please don't let her look in here, he prayed.

"Where does this lead to?" she asked.

"It don't lead nowhere, madam," Bert answered. "That there's a wardrobe."

"A what?"

"Where the artistes hang up their things."

"Oh, a clothes closet."

"S'right."

"Let's take a look inside, shall we?"

Sparrow shrank back even further as the door started to open. Then it stopped at the sound of a new voice – the unmistakable, plummy tones of Mr Trump. Sparrow had never thought he would be pleased to hear the theatre manager's voice, but he was now.

"May I enquire as to what is transpiring here?" Mr Trump asked.

"Oh, Mr Trump, sir," Bert stammered. "I can explain."

"You'd better, Bertram. And your explanation had better be good."

"Oh, please, sir," the woman said, sounding as sweet as honey. "Don't be hard on him. It's all my fault. You see, I lost something very precious in your theatre last evening, and this dear man was helping me look for it."

"In a dressing room? At the scene of a gruesome murder?"

"I handed it to Mr Marvin during the show,

for his little girl to identify, and somehow he never got around to returning it."

"Why did you not ask him for it last night?"

"I would have, but when I tried to come backstage…" She broke off, and began sobbing. "Oh, it was just too, too awful…"

"Yes, yes," Mr Trump said, clearly embarrassed. "Pray don't distress yourself. What exactly was it you were seeking?"

"A locket, a dear little golden locket. I'm sure it was an oversight on Mr Marvin's part not to return it, and I have no wish to involve the police, with all the bad publicity it would bring to the theatre …"

"The police searched this room most thoroughly last night, madam. I fear your locket could not be here. Perhaps it was dropped elsewhere in the theatre – in the auditorium, say. I shall instruct my cleaning staff to be especially vigilant in keeping a lookout for it."

"Thank you. You are most kind."

"Not at all. Now, Bertram, if you would secure this room again, and give me the key, I shall escort this lady from the premises."

Sparrow heard the door close and the lock turn.

Then there was silence and he could breathe again. His head was spinning. He couldn't wait to tell Wiggins and Mary what he had just heard. He jumped out of the cupboard and dashed across the room, opened the window and climbed out. Then he hurried home to HQ as fast as his legs could carry him, with never a backward glance.

Mary was brushing Queenie's hair and showing her how she would change the style for the stage, when Sparrow burst in. None of the others were back yet, and the two girls were startled by his sudden appearance.

"Oooh, Sparrow!" Queenie cried. "You give us a fright comin' in like that. What you do that for?"

"I found somethin'…" he gasped, out of breath, "I found somethin' out. Listen…"

But before Sparrow could go on, he heard a noise behind him. Queenie shrieked and pointed. Turning round, he saw a man standing in the doorway. The bearded man with the limp.

"It's the murderer!" Sparrow yelled.

"Mary!" the man shouted.

Mary screamed, went white, and fainted.

EIGHT

Wiggins and the rest of the search party arrived back at HQ to find the bearded man bending over Mary, who was now lying on a bed, just coming round from her faint.

"It's him!" Wiggins shouted. "Quick, Beav – run and get a copper! It's the murderer!"

"No, no!" Mary called, trying to sit up. "He's not a murderer. He's my daddy."

She flung her arms around the man and hugged and kissed him, and he hugged and kissed her back, and they both wept tears of happiness. The Boys were dumbfounded. Their mouths fell open as they tried to take in this amazing news.

"But … but…" Beaver babbled. "You can't be. You're dead…"

"Do I look dead?" the man said, over Mary's

shoulder. "My name is Jack Elliot, and this is my little girl."

"What are you doing here?" Wiggins asked. "How did you find this place?"

"I found out Mary had disappeared from the theatre, and I had an idea you lot might have something to do with it," he replied. "So I followed this young man." He nodded at Sparrow. "He was in such a hurry he never looked behind him – unlike you and your friend when I tried to follow you."

"Sparrow!" Wiggins rebuked him. "How many times have I told you…"

"He nearly lost me more than once, mind. I had the dickens of a job keeping up with him." He patted his lame leg. "I don't move so fast since my accident."

"Oh, Daddy," Mary said. "They told us you'd been killed."

"I very nearly was," her father replied, stroking her head lovingly. "But when I thought I'd never see you and your ma again, I just hung on and hung on and refused to die. And now here I am at last. Too late for your poor dear ma, I know, but I thank God you're safe and sound."

"But what took you so long?" Wiggins asked.

"Yeah – why did you let her think you was dead?" Beaver joined in accusingly.

"I didn't have any choice," Mr Elliot answered. "I was too ill. And anyway I was hundreds of miles away from them – thousands of miles even – out in the wilderness of the Yukon."

"What happened?"

"My partner and I were digging a mine, searching for gold. A rival prospector tried to get rid of us so he could grab our claim. He blew up our mine with us inside it. When our friends dug us out, my partner was dead and I was in a bad way. Nobody expected me to live through the night. I guess that's how word got back to New York that I'd died. I was unconscious for days, and when I finally did come round, I didn't know who I was or where I was. My brain was hurt as bad as my legs. It took months before I could move or think straight. As soon as I could, I sent messages to Mary and her ma, telling them what had happened. But none of them ever arrived. Somebody in New York made sure they never saw them."

"Marvin!" exclaimed Mary.

"Very likely," her father said. "That man was a

scoundrel through and through."

"Is that why you killed him?" Wiggins asked.

"I didn't kill him."

"We saw you, bending over his body."

"He was dead when I found him. Somebody had got there first."

"Why'd you run off, then?" asked Beaver.

"Because I knew nobody would believe I hadn't done it."

"That's true," said Wiggins. "'Specially if they knowed you'd trailed him all the way from New York, right?"

"Right. You're not stupid, are you? In fact, I'd say you were a pretty smart lad."

"Comes of working for Mr Sherlock Holmes," Wiggins said with a grin. "I learnt a lot from him."

"Sherlock Holmes? You work for Mr Holmes, you say?"

"We're the Baker Street Boys, Mr Holmes's Irregulars as he sometimes calls us."

"Well, I never. Will you take me to him?"

"Sorry," said Wiggins, shaking his head. "Can't. He's away on a case. You'll have to make do with his assistants. That's us."

"I see. Well, I suppose I could do worse."

"Right then, you'd better sit down and tell us the rest of it."

Wiggins gestured to his special chair. Mr Elliot looked at the rickety piece of furniture dubiously, then lowered himself gently into it, half afraid that it would break under his weight. Fortunately it didn't, even when Mary sat on his lap.

"Like I said," he told the Boys, "it took months and months before I was well enough to make the journey back East. And when I got to New York I discovered my lovely wife had married Marvin, and then taken sick and died."

"But why had she married him?" Queenie asked.

"She needed someone to look after her and Mary, I guess. She thought I was dead, remember."

"We all did," said Mary, sobbing at the memory. "And he could be real nice – when he wanted to be."

"Anyway, by the time I got there, he'd disappeared, and taken my little girl with him. Nobody seemed to know where he was, so I hired the Pinkerton Detective Agency to find him. And they discovered that he wasn't just a phoney in the theatre, pretending to read minds and all that. He was a crook as well."

"I knew it!" said Wiggins. "What did he do?"

"He was a member of a gang of criminals who carried out a whole lot of big robberies. But he double-crossed the others, and took the loot for himself. When they went after him, he hid the stuff and vamoosed across the Atlantic. The Pinkerton men thought he'd been helped by a mysterious British mastermind."

"Moriarty!" the Boys shouted, all together.

"Who's Moriarty?" Mr Elliot asked.

"The Napoleon of crime, according to Mr Holmes," Wiggins replied. "He says he's the most dangerous man in London."

"You've had dealings with him?"

"We have crossed swords with him," Wiggins said, trying to sound nonchalant.

"And we won!" Shiner cried.

"I seen 'im with Marvin the other night," said Sparrow. "I bet they was up to no good."

"I'll wager you're right," said Mr Elliot.

"What was Marvin's racket in the States?" Wiggins asked.

"He got into rich people's houses to give private performances and fake séances, claiming to make contact with their dead relatives. Once he was there, he'd look around and see where all the most valuable things were, then go back afterwards and steal them. Or send somebody else to do it."

"Oh, no!" Mary let out an agonized cry. "That's what we were doing here – holding séances in rich people's houses!"

"And stealing their stuff?" Gertie asked. "That's a terrible thing to do."

There was silence as the Boys all looked at Mary with mixed feelings. She burst into tears.

"I didn't know about the stealing," she sobbed. "I swear I didn't."

"Of course you didn't," her father said, holding her tight.

"I believe you," said Sparrow, almost too brightly.

But some of the other Boys were not so sure.

"You must have knowed," Shiner accused her. "'Ow could you not have knowed what he was up to?"

"Hang on! Hang on!" Sparrow shouted. "Think about it. It's obvious!"

"What is?" Wiggins asked.

The others waited expectantly while Sparrow made the most of the moment.

"Hypnotism!" he declared, after a dramatic pause. "Marvin hypnotized Mary – and her ma afore her – to make 'em do what he wanted and then forget all about it so they couldn't never split on him."

Shiner and Gertie pooh-poohed the idea, but when Sparrow reminded everyone how Mary had not remembered talking to him that time, and how he had watched Marvin put Rosie into a trance, they all began to take him seriously.

"Yeah," said Wiggins, "but how can we find out? How does it work?"

Sparrow described how Marvin had told Rosie that after he had hypnotized her once, he could put her under again just by saying the magic words and clicking his fingers.

"What are the magic words?" Wiggins asked. "P'raps if we could put Mary under, she might be able to remember things."

Sparrow shook his head. He couldn't recall what Marvin had said.

"Abracadabra?" Beaver suggested helpfully.

"I seen a conjuror say that once."

"No," Sparrow replied. "Nothin' like that."

He racked his brain. "I keep thinkin' about ice cream…'

"You would," Shiner scoffed. "Always thinkin' of your belly!"

"Listen to who's talkin'!" Sparrow retorted.

"'Stop me and buy one?'" Gertie suggested.

"No. It was sort of foreign-soundin'. And two words."

"Hokey-pokey?" asked Queenie, echoing the cry of the Italian ice-cream sellers on the streets of London.

"Yeah, somethin' like that," said Sparrow. And then his face cleared.

"Hocus-pocus!" he yelled. "That's what it was! Hocus-pocus!"

They all looked expectantly at Mary. But nothing happened. Wiggins repeated the words to her, but still they had no effect. Then Sparrow remembered.

"You gotta click your fingers as well," he said.

Wiggins said the magic words again, and tried to click his fingers. But he couldn't get them to make a sound, and Mary shook her head sadly.

"Nothing," she said. "I don't feel any different."

Wiggins turned to Mr Elliot.

"Can you click your fingers?" he asked.

"I think so," Mr Elliot answered, and did so.

"Right," said Wiggins. "After I say the words… Hocus-pocus!"

Mr Elliot clicked his fingers again, more loudly. Immediately, Mary jerked her head and stared straight in front of her. She was in a trance. The Boys gazed at her – and Wiggins – in amazement. Sparrow beamed with pride.

"Well, I never," said Mr Elliot. He passed his hand up and down in front of his daughter's face. She did not blink or show any sign that she could see it.

"What do we do now?" asked Wiggins.

"Ask her things," said Queenie. "Go on – ask her about Marvin."

Wiggins cleared his throat nervously.

"Can you hear me, Mary?" he said.

"I hear you and will obey," she replied in a strange, flat voice.

"Crikey," said Wiggins. "Er, Mary, do you remember what Marvin told you to do when you went into people's houses?"

"Yes. Marvin said he would tell me what to say when we got there. He told me that when I woke up I would forget where we had been and what I had said. He told me these were secret and I was to keep all his secrets and not tell nobody."

"Brilliant," said Beaver. "Just like Sparrow said!"

"Is that all he told you?" Wiggins continued.

"He told me I must keep my ma's gold locket safe. I must keep it with me always."

"The locket!" Sparrow exclaimed, suddenly remembering what had happened in the dressing room. "The locket – that's what it's all about!"

"Sssshhh!" Queenie hissed at him. Don't disturb her. It might be dangerous."

"Yeah, but—"

"Shh! Later!"

"I think that's enough for the moment," said Mr Elliot, worried that his daughter might be harmed. "She's proved the point. Now bring her back."

"Right," said Wiggins, a bit disappointed as he was just getting into it. "OK, Mary. You can wake up now."

Mary did not move, or show any sign of emerging from her trance.

"Wake up, Mary," he repeated. "Time to wake up."

Still she stared straight ahead of her. Wiggins squeezed her hand, then patted her gently on the cheek, but she didn't move a muscle. He started to panic slightly. What if he couldn't bring her round? What if she were stuck like this for ever?

"Oh, Lor," he muttered. "Now what do I do?"

Sparrow thought frantically, trying for all he was worth to recall what Marvin had done. He realized that he had seen Marvin put Rosie *into* a trance but could not remember how he had brought her out of it. Then he recalled the performance on-stage. Although the trance had been fake, Marvin might have done the same as he would with the real thing. But what exactly had he done? Sparrow closed his eyes and pictured the act. Suddenly, he saw it.

"You have to count her down," he said.

"What d'you mean?" Wiggins asked.

"You have to say you're gonna count down from five to nothin' and when you get to one she'll be awake."

Wiggins looked into Mary's eyes again.

"Mary," he said, "I am going to count down from five to nothing…"

"And when you get to one…" Sparrow prompted impatiently.

"And when I get to one, you will be awake."

He counted, loudly and slowly. When he finished, there was a moment's silence as everyone held their breath. Then Mary blinked her eyes and looked around.

"Why are you all staring at me?" she asked. "Did it work?"

"It worked," her father told her, and embraced her.

"Marvin *did* make you forget everythin'," Queenie told her, "just like Sparrow said."

"You never knowed what you was doin'," Beaver added. "So nobody can blame you."

Mary turned to Sparrow, with tears of joy in her eyes.

"Thank you, Sparrow," she said. "You're my hero."

And she kissed him, making him turn bright crimson.

"We ain't finished yet," he said. "We still gotta find Rosie."

"That's right," Queenie said. "We still got no idea where she is."

"And we gotta find out about that an' all," said Sparrow, pointing to the locket hanging round Mary's neck. "It might give us a clue."

"Why should it do that?" Wiggins asked.

Sparrow proceeded to tell the others about the American woman he had heard in Marvin's dressing room, and how she had been searching for the locket.

"She never gave no locket to Marvin," he said when he'd finished. "I'd have seen. I reckon it was this one she was after."

"You could be right," said Wiggins. "But why would anybody go to that sort of trouble to get it? Let's have a look at it, Mary."

Mary slipped the chain over her head and handed the locket to him. The others clustered around as he examined it.

"It's very pretty and all that," he said, "but it ain't exac'ly that precious, is it? Not like if it was covered in diamonds and stuff... D'you know anything about it, Mr Elliot?"

He handed the locket to Mary's father, who opened it and looked at the picture inside, then shook his head.

"I've never seen it before," he said. "And I've no idea who this lady might be."

"You mean it ain't Mary's granny?"

"No. Whoever she is, she is most certainly not Mary's grandmamma."

Wiggins took the locket back, scratched his head, and stared intently at the little portrait as though willing it to speak. If Mr Elliot had not been there, he would have sat down in his chair, put on his deerstalker hat and clamped his pipe between his teeth while he pondered on the problem. Instead, he could only pace to and fro along the cellar floor, holding the locket in his hand while the others watched and waited. Suddenly his face lit up. He hurried to the table and laid the locket down on it. Taking out his penknife, he carefully poked the point behind the picture and levered it out.

"Aha!" he said in his best Sherlock Holmes manner. "What have we here?"

Tucked in the back of the locket behind the picture was a small piece of paper, neatly folded to fit into the small space. Like a magician performing a special trick, Wiggins lifted it out, opened it and placed it on the table.

"What is it?" asked Beaver.

Wiggins frowned. He really didn't know what the paper was. But Mr Elliot did. Reaching over to pick it up and look at it more closely, he said, "It's a ticket for a safety deposit or a left-luggage office."

Most of the Boys looked disappointed.

"Ooh," Shiner groaned. "I thought it might be somethin' important."

"It is," said Wiggins, his eyes shining with excitement. "Now we know where Marvin stashed the loot from the robberies. This is what the murderers was after. This is what they killed Marvin for. And this is why they snatched Rosie."

Beaver looked puzzled,

"Why's that?" he asked.

"Don't you see?" said Wiggins. "They thought she was Mary."

Mary put her hands to her face in shock.

"...and that she'd have the locket round her neck!" she cried.

"Oh, no!" Queenie gasped. "What they gonna do to her now they know she ain't?"

NINE

The excitement the Boys had felt when they solved the mystery of Mary's locket soon gave way to deep gloom. It was obvious that Rosie really was in the hands of a ruthless gang. They had no clues as to where she was being held – and no one could forget that the criminals had already killed Marvin.

"It's time to call in the police," Mr Elliot said. "I must give myself up."

"But they'll chuck you in jail," Wiggins protested. "They think you're the murderer."

"Precisely," Mr Elliot replied. "And while they're wasting time looking for me, they're not looking for the real killers."

"Nor for Rosie," said Queenie.

"What if they don't believe you?" asked Gertie. "The coppers never believed my da' when he told 'em he was innocent."

"We'll all come with you," Sparrow chirped, "and tell 'em what really happened. We'll make 'em believe you."

"That's right," Mary joined in. "We'll give them the locket and the ticket and all."

"Fine," said Beaver, "but how's it gonna help us find Rosie?"

"I'll tell you how," said Wiggins. He had just had a brainwave, and his eyes were shining. "We can't go to the crooks, 'cos we dunno where they are, right?"

"Right," Beaver replied glumly.

"So we get the crooks to come to us!"

"How are you going to do that?" asked Mr Elliot.

"With this," said Wiggins, and he picked up the ticket. "They've come all the way from America for this – and killed Marvin for it and kidnapped Rosie. So they must want it pretty bad."

"Yeah," said Shiner. "If they done all that, what they gonna do to us when they find out we got it?"

"Shiner's right," said Beaver. "How we gonna keep it quiet?"

"We ain't," Wiggins replied. "We're gonna set a trap with this as the bait."

The Boys all gazed at Wiggins in admiration. Yet again he had come up with a brilliant idea worthy of Mr Holmes himself.

"Excellent," said Mr Elliot. "But how can you be so sure they'll come for it?"

"They think it's still inside the locket, don't they?" Wiggins replied. "And they don't know that we knows about it. So all we gotta do is sort of dangle the locket in front of 'em, and they'll come running."

"And how are you going to dangle it in front of them?"

"Ah, that's where we're gonna need a bit of help."

"From whom?"

"From Inspector Lestrade. Come on, everybody – down to Scotland Yard. Quick!"

It was hard to convince Inspector Lestrade that Mr Elliot had not murdered Marvin. As the inspector said, he had a very good motive for wanting to kill the man who had taken his wife and daughter from him, and he had, after all, followed him all the way to London. But eventually, with the help of Mary and the Boys, Mr Elliot managed to persuade Lestrade that he was innocent and that Marvin had already been dead when he found him. Sparrow's report of the American woman searching for the locket was a great help, especially since it could be corroborated by Bert and Mr Trump. And the ticket that Wiggins had found hidden inside it was final proof.

"All you've got to do now, Inspector," said Mr Elliot, "is find that woman."

"And the man what gave Marvin the black spot," added Sparrow.

"*Now* what are you on about?" sighed Lestrade, staring at him as though he was mad.

Sparrow reached into his pocket, produced the piece of paper with the bloodstain on it, and handed it over.

"What's this?" the inspector asked, wrinkling his nose in distaste.

"Don't you remember?" said Sparrow. "It was in the dressing room, by the body. You didn't think it was anythin' important."

"But it is," Wiggins told him. "It's the black spot."

"Like in *Treasure Island*," Queenie added. "Ain't you never read *Treasure Island*, Inspector?'"

"Er, no," Lestrade admitted. "I don't have

time for fairy tales."

"Oh, it ain't a fairy tale," Queenie said. "It's all about pirates and buried treasure and suchlike. You oughta read it."

"I told you, young lady, I don't have time for such frivolities. Now kindly stop wasting my precious time."

His face was turning quite red with indignation, but Queenie was unperturbed.

"It's a wonderful story," she went on, and proceeded to tell him all about the black spot and what it meant. When she had finished, Sparrow told him how he had seen a man in the audience hand the paper to Marvin, and how Marvin had looked very scared.

"Why did you not tell me all this back at the theatre?" Lestrade demanded angrily. "Don't you know it's an offence to withhold information from a police officer?"

"I tried to, but you wouldn't listen. And you said the paper didn't mean nothin'."

Lestrade's face turned even redder.

"Humph!" he spluttered. "That was then. It now appears from fresh evidence that we are looking for two people. At least."

"Don't worry, Inspector," Wiggins reassured him. "We'll help you find 'em."

Lestrade did not seem to be soothed by Wiggins's offer. In fact, he looked as though he was about to explode with exasperation. But Wiggins just grinned cheekily at him.

"Here's what we're gonna do," he said, and began to outline his plan. At first the inspector was very doubtful, but by the time Wiggins had finished, with enthusiastic support from Mr Elliot, he was almost won round.

"It is very, er, unorthodox," he grumbled. "The sort of stunt that your friend Mr Holmes might try. But it just might work. Are you quite sure, though, that you could play your part?"

"Certain sure, guv'nor," Wiggins answered. "Trust me."

"And I'll be helping him," said Mary.

Lestrade looked at their two eager young faces, then sighed and nodded. "Very well," he pronounced. "I may come to regret it, but I agree."

The next day, all the newspapers in London carried reports on their front pages saying that Mary had been found, alive and well. Most of them had a picture of her, wearing her locket round her neck. Inspector Lestrade had circulated this news and the picture to the editors, asking them to report that she would be giving a special performance at the Imperial Music Hall that night. The proceeds, it was announced, would be used to pay for her to return home to America.

Wiggins and Lestrade had had to let Mr Trump into the secret – they would not have been able to use his theatre without his agreement. He had not been keen at first, even though he knew that the theatre would be packed. He soon changed his mind, however, when he was told that the ticket money would not really be used to pay for Mary's fare and that he would be able to keep it all. After that he became very enthusiastic, happy at the thought of all the free publicity the Imperial would be getting. Only one thing still worried him.

"Who will be taking poor Mr Marvin's place in the act?" he asked.

To the manager's horror, Wiggins stepped forward.

"I will," he said.

"You?! How can you possibly…?"

"S'all right – Mary's gonna learn me."

"Mary's going to teach you," Mr Trump corrected him automatically.

"That's what I said. She's gonna learn me all about it. Like she did with Rosie."

"Humph," Mr Trump snorted. "I always suspected there was something underhand transpiring in that respect."

"Worked, though, didn't it?"

"Only too well," Mr Trump admitted. "If she had not been quite so convincing, the villains would not have mistaken her for Mary."

"Don't worry," Lestrade said, "I don't think anyone will mistake young Wiggins for Mr Marvin. And in any case, I shall have men posted throughout the theatre, keeping their eyes open for our villains."

For the rest of that day, and most of the night, Wiggins and Mary practised and rehearsed. And when they woke up the next day after only a few hours' sleep, they practised and rehearsed again, this time in the theatre, until Wiggins was word-perfect. The only breaks they had were for quick meals and costume fittings. Although Rosie had been wearing Mary's best costume, Mary had a spare one, which was still hanging in the dressing-room cupboard. But Wiggins had nothing, and finding an evening-dress suit for him, complete with tailcoat and bow tie, was a problem – all the suits in the shops were for adult men, and would have been too big for him even if they were cut down.

It was Mr Trump who found the solution; he borrowed a suit from a famous woman performer who dressed up as a man in her act, and who was only slightly taller than Wiggins. It was a bit baggy for him, particularly around the chest and bottom, but that was soon put right with the help of a few safety pins and a clothes peg. With his hair plastered down with brilliantine he was ready to face the audience, looking every inch the seasoned performer.

The first part of the evening passed off uneventfully, with all the usual turns doing their stuff and enjoying the buzz of excitement in the theatre, even though they knew the excitement was not for them. Sparrow peered at the audience through the spy hole at the side of the stage, doing his best to remember what the man who had given Marvin the bloodstained paper looked like, and trying to see if he could spot him anywhere. He thought he saw someone like him standing at the back of the stalls, near the bar – but when he pointed out the man to Lestrade, the inspector told him that was one of his policemen in plain clothes. In fact, several of the more suspicious-looking characters in the audience turned out to be policemen in disguise. Sparrow gave up pointing them out when Lestrade began to get annoyed and stomped off to check on the men he had posted outside the theatre.

At last it was time for Wiggins and Mary to make their appearance. Behind the heavy red velvet curtain, Mary sat on a small golden chair in the centre of the stage, surrounded by potted palms. Wiggins took up his position at her shoulder while Mr Trump walked out in front of the curtain and called for a minute's silence in memory of the murdered Marvin. The audience was suitably hushed, with most people bowing their heads and managing to look solemn for a full sixty seconds.

Then Mr Trump noisily cleared his throat and held

out his arms. "Thank you, ladies and gentlemen!" he boomed. "And now, for your delectation, it is the Imperial Music Hall's proud privilege to present to you a young lady who has displayed fantabulous fortitude following the tragic demise of her beloved paterfamilias and partner in performance, known to you as Mystic Marvin. By the greatest of good fortune, to support her tonight we have been able to call on the services of a remarkable young noviciate in the psychic skills of telepathic transcendentalism, a worthy successor to Mystic Marvin himself. Ladies and gentlemen, I give you, for the first time on any public platform, Little Mary, Clairvoyant Extraordinaire, and the Amazing Arnoldo!"

The orchestra sounded a loud chord, followed by a long drum roll and a crash of cymbals, and the curtain rose to a burst of polite applause from the audience. The first sight of the packed house made Wiggins's knees shake and his hands tremble with nerves. He was suddenly conscious that some of the brilliantine on his hair was melting in the heat of the stage lights and running down the side of his cheek, mingling with the perspiration on his face before trickling down his neck and into his collar. For a second or two he wanted to run off the stage and hide in the wings, but he gripped the back of Mary's chair with one hand and bowed low to acknowledge the applause. Then he took a deep breath, stepped forward and held up one hand.

"Good evening, ladies and gentlemen," he began, trying to pitch his voice to reach the very back of the theatre, as Mary had taught him that afternoon. "My name is Arnoldo and this is my assistant, the lovely Little Mary. Tonight we will demonstrate to you the amazing powers of mentalism. In order to achieve this, I shall begin by hypnotizing Mary, so that her mind is completely receptive to the messages which I shall transmit to her."

There was an expectant murmuring from the audience, and Wiggins held up his hand to stop it before continuing with Marvin's patter.

"Ladies and gentlemen," he announced. "I must ask for complete silence while I induce a hypnotic trance in Mary. Any disturbance at this time – any disturbance whatsoever – could be highly danger-ous to her."

He leant over Mary and very deliberately lifted the locket and its chain from around her neck, then held it up to make sure everyone could see it clearly before he started swinging it before her eyes like a pendulum. Once she was supposedly hypnotized and he had performed the trick with the long sharp pin, he replaced the locket around her neck, again taking care that everyone could see it.

With the act under way, Wiggins found that he was actually beginning to enjoy himself, and he was soon climbing down from the stage and moving among the audience asking for objects for Mary to identify. He was doing so well that all eyes were on him as he held up each object and called out the coded words with complete confidence. So nobody noticed when one of the men who were standing at the bar put down his glass and slipped quietly away.

The policeman on duty in the alleyway behind the dressing rooms was feeling cold and bored. He had been watching and waiting all evening. Nothing had happened, he had seen nobody and he was sure he would not see anybody. This whole thing was a wild goose chase, he thought, and he would be glad when it was over and he could get back to the police station and a warm fire.

He perked up when a man came round the corner and approached him with a friendly smile.

"Constable," the man said, addressing him with
the voice of authority. "Any sign?"

"No, sir. Quiet as the grave."

"Good. I have a message for you from the inspect-
or. You're to report to him at the stage door."

"What, now, sir?"

"That's right. I'll keep watch here 'til you get
back."

The policeman nodded, pleased to have the
tedium relieved. He began walking off – but as soon
as he had passed, the man leapt at him. Moving like
lightning, he pulled a cosh from his pocket, knocked
off the policeman's helmet and cracked him over the
back of the head. The policeman fell to the ground,
unconscious. In a few seconds, he was bound,
gagged and dragged into a dark corner. The man
glanced quickly around, then proceeded silently
towards the dressing-room window.

TEN

Wiggins and Mary finished their act to the sound of great applause, bowed to the audience, then walked off the stage as the curtain fell. Wiggins was so elated by their success that for a moment he quite forgot why they had been doing it. So did the other Boys, who had been watching from the wings and now clustered around them offering their congratulations. They were soon brought down to earth, however, as Inspector Lestrade greeted Wiggins with a sour face.

"I knew it wouldn't work," he said in a told-you-so kind of voice.

"You ain't seen nobody, then?" Wiggins asked.

"Not a soul. Complete waste of time."

"Hang on," Wiggins replied, "the night ain't over yet. You gotta let the dog see the rabbit."

"And what is that supposed to mean?"

"Well, we flashed the locket so everybody could see it. Now we gotta give 'em the chance to try and collect it."

"While you two are arguing," Mary interrupted impatiently, "I'm going to get changed."

She hurried off to the dressing room and closed the door behind her. A moment later, a piercing scream came from inside the room. It was Mary's voice. Wiggins beat everyone in the race to the door, but it was locked from the inside. Lestrade joined him and Beaver in putting their shoulders to it. After three attempts, it splintered under their combined weight and crashed open. Inside, Mary was lying on the floor, clutching at her neck where the locket had been torn off.

"Look after Mary," Wiggins yelled at Queenie and Sparrow as he dashed across the room to the open window.

At the end of the alley he could see a man just disappearing round the corner. Wiggins climbed out and gave chase, the tails of his evening coat flying out behind him, as Beaver, Gertie and Shiner scrambled through the window and joined in. As they rounded the corner they were just in time to see the man being driven off in one of the cabs that were always waiting outside the stage door. They tried to catch it, but it had too much of a start and they were forced to turn back.

There was only one other cab waiting. They rushed up to it – but there was no driver to be seen. He was sheltering from the cold inside the theatre, enjoying a baked potato and a chat with Bert. Wiggins let out a yell of frustration, but Gertie was already climbing up into the driver's seat.

"Get in!" she shouted. "We'll catch 'em yet!"

"Can you drive this?" Wiggins asked.

"Sure. Didn't I grow up in a caravan?" she replied. "Get aboard! Quick!"

Wiggins needed no second bidding. He, Beaver and Shiner piled into the cab as Gertie grabbed the reins, cracked the whip and ordered the horse to "Giddup!" In seconds they were careering along the street in hot pursuit of the other cab. Behind them, the driver came tumbling out of the stage door, shouting, "Stop, thief! Stop them! STOP, THIEF!" Lestrade, who was too old and too slow to climb through the dressing-room window, emerged from the door alongside him, tore off his bowler hat and flung it to the ground in rage.

Gertie had not driven for ages, but she had been taught well by her father and had not forgotten the skills they had practised together at gypsy horse fairs. There was little traffic on the London streets at that time of night, and she soon whipped up the cab horse from a fast trot to a canter and very nearly a gallop. While she whooped with delight and shouted encouragement to the horse, the Boys inside clung on desperately as the cab swayed and rattled and skittered over the cobbles, its iron-shod wheels striking showers of sparks from the stones.

But no matter how fast and furiously Gertie drove, the other cab had too much of a head start and there were too many turnings and junctions for her to keep it in sight. When they came to a crossroads there was no sign of it, and nothing to tell them which way it had gone. Gertie pulled the horse to a halt.

"It's no use," she called to Wiggins. "We've lost 'em. I'm sorry."

To everyone's surprise, Wiggins did not seem particularly upset.

"Don't worry," he told Gertie. "You did your best."

"Yeah. That was t'rific," Shiner said. "Better even than them horseless carriages in Windsor. Ain't that right, Beav?"

Beaver was still trying to get his breath back, and it took a few moments before he could say anything.

"What we gonna do now, Wiggins?" he gasped. "Which way we gonna go?"

"No way," Wiggins answered. "We wait here."

"Wait? What for?"

"For that," said Wiggins, pointing down a street, where the first cab was just coming back into view round a corner.

The driver waved his whip and beckoned to them.

"What's he doin'?" Gertie asked.

"You'll see. Go on, drive down there."

Gertie started the horse again, and they trundled down to the other cab.

As they drew level with it, the driver called out to them. "It worked! We've got them!"

Wiggins grinned at him and the others stared as they saw his face and heard his voice. It was Jack Elliot, Mary's father.

The two cabs pulled up outside a house.

"This is where I dropped him," Mr Elliot said. "He's in there."

They all climbed out and crept silently to the house. The curtains in the front room were drawn, but a chink of light shone through a small gap between them. Wiggins moved to the window and peeped in. A man and a woman were bending over something on the table and the man was holding a vicious-looking knife. Wiggins turned, nodded vigorously to the others, and made a sign towards the door. Mr Elliot tried the handle. It turned. He eased the door open and they all tiptoed in.

The man was using the knife to prise open the locket when the door to the room opened and Wiggins and Mr Elliot burst in, with Beaver, Gertie and Shiner close behind them.

"What the...?" the man snarled in a heavy American accent. "Who the devil are you?"

"What d'you want?" the woman asked. "You can't come bustin' into decent law-abidin' folks' houses like this."

"I've a good mind to call the cops," the man joined in.

"No need," said Mr Elliot. "They're already on their way."

"Whaddya mean?"

"Why don't you read what's on that?" Wiggins said, pointing to the piece of paper the man had just taken from the locket.

The man hesitated, then unfolded the paper and smoothed it out. Written on it was a simple message: "The game is up." The man's eyes blazed and his face turned purple with fury.

"Why, you…!" he roared, grabbing his knife and starting towards Wiggins.

"Stop that!" a new voiced barked. "Stop right there! You are under arrest. Both of you."

Lestrade strode into the room, followed by two burly police constables.

"I'll take that, if you don't mind," Lestrade said, reaching for the knife. "You will be charged with murder, robbery and kidnapping."

"Kidnapping?" the man said. "Don't know what you're talking about."

"Where is she?" Wiggins demanded.

"Yeah, where's Rosie?" Beaver joined in.

"Listen!" Gertie called out. "Can you hear something?"

They all stopped talking and listened. From the next room came a muffled cry. Beaver reached the door first, and flung it open. Rosie, still wearing Mary's stage costume, was lying on a bare bed, her hands and feet bound with rope and her mouth gagged with a strip of once-white cloth. Beaver untied the gag while Gertie released her hands and feet.

"You all right?" Beaver asked anxiously.

"I am now," Rosie replied, sitting up and flexing her stiff limbs. "You didn't half take your time getting 'ere. I'm famished!"

"Well, we're here now," said Wiggins from the doorway. "And so is half of Scotland Yard, so you're safe and sound."

Gertie put her arms round Rosie, and gave her a comforting hug. Then she helped her to stand, and led her through into the other room, where the police were handcuffing the American couple.

"Ah, Rosie," Inspector Lestrade greeted her. "Are you all right? Did they harm you?"

"Not really," Rosie replied. "Not me. But they killed poor old Marvin – leastways, *he* did." She pointed at the man, who glowered at her sullenly. "Stuck him with a dirty great knife, he did. In the back an' all, the brute."

"And you witnessed this?" Lestrade asked her.

"Dunno about that, but I seen it. I seen it all – afore he chucked a blanket over me head and carted me off here."

"Excellent," said Lestrade, beaming happily. "I believe that wraps it all up very nicely. Yet another triumph for Scotland Yard."

Mr Elliot cleared his throat noisily. "With just a *little* help from the Baker Street Boys," he said.

Lestrade's smile shrivelled like a dried prune. "Of course," he said. "We professionals are always gratified to acknowledge the assistance of members of the public."

"Cor blimey," said Wiggins with a broad grin. "He sounds just like Mr Trump, don't he?"

Sherlock Holmes and Dr Watson had arrived back in London that same evening, and Wiggins reported to Mr Holmes first thing the next morning. The great detective was most impressed by what he heard, and congratulated Wiggins and the Boys on their achievement in trapping the murderer. He was particularly pleased to learn that they had foiled his great adversary, Moriarty, and was keen to hear all about this part of the case. When Wiggins had finished, he patted him on the shoulder, said, "Well done, my boy. Well done, indeed," and gave him a whole gold sovereign as a reward.

That afternoon, all the Boys, well scrubbed and wearing their best clothes, were ushered into a luxury suite in the Grand Metropolitan Hotel. Mr Elliot had moved into the hotel with Mary, and had invited the Boys to a slap-up tea party to thank them for all they had done for his daughter, and to celebrate their latest achievement. A long table had been set up in the drawing room, piled high with scrumptious food – iced cakes and buns, jam tarts and custard pies, chocolate eclairs oozing cream, delicious fruit trifles, sausage rolls and sandwiches of every description – as well as giant jugs of ginger beer and lemonade and, especially for Sparrow and Mary, dandelion and burdock. It was a feast fit for heroes, and the Boys tucked into it with gusto.

Towards the end of the party, there was a knock at the door and Mr Holmes was shown in. After he had introduced himself to Mr Elliot and expressed his admiration for the spread that the Boys were attacking so heartily, he walked over to speak to them.

"I have no wish to interrupt the festivities," he said, "so I will be brief. I have information which I think you might like to know – especially you, my good friend Beaver, before you begin making a record of this latest adventure."

"How did you know I—?" Beaver began to ask, but Mr Holmes just smiled mysteriously and tapped the side of his nose with his forefinger.

"Since speaking to Wiggins this morning," he went on, "I have been making certain enquiries, and I have been able to deduce that Marvin and Moriarty were hatching a plot to deceive one of the noblest ladies in the land in a most cruel fashion. May I see the locket that lies at the centre of this intrigue, if you please?"

Mr Elliot produced the locket from his waistcoat pocket and handed it to him. Mr Holmes clicked it open and looked at the picture inside.

"As I thought," he declared. "This is a portrait of the Countess of Loamshire. Moriarty's sinister plot was to use Marvin to gain access to the countess through one of his fake séances, when the poor lady might easily be persuaded that Mary was her long-lost granddaughter. The little girl was drowned, together with her parents, in a yachting accident off the coast of America, but the bodies were never recovered and the countess always cherished the hope that at least one of them might have survived, perhaps on some remote island."

"Oh, how dreadful," Mary cried. "Why would Moriarty and Marvin do such a terrible thing?"

"Money," Mr Holmes replied. "The countess is immensely rich, and as her only grandchild you would have been the sole heiress to the Loamshire fortune."

"But I wouldn't do it! I'd never do such a thing."

"Who knows what you might do under the influence of hypnosis? I have no doubt that once you had been successfully installed, the old lady's life would have been a very short one."

"You mean they'd have killed her?"

"I do indeed. And you, too, once you had inherited and they had bled you dry."

"Oh, how horrible. How absolutely horrible!"

"That is the most dastardly thing I have ever heard," Mr Elliot exploded. "To think those villains were using my little girl for such a purpose…"

"Fortunately they were thwarted," Mr Holmes said. "By the actions of my brave Irregulars."

He stretched out his hand and picked up a glass from the table.

"A toast," he said. "I raise my glass to the Baker Street Boys!"

"Amen to that," said Mr Elliot, grabbing a glass for himself.

They both drank. A smile spread slowly across Mr Holmes's face as the taste brought back memories of his childhood.

"Ah, dandelion and burdock," he said dreamily. "And an excellent vintage!"

After draining his glass, Mr Holmes headed for the door, saying he would leave the Boys to their festivities. But as he opened it, he saw an elderly man and woman approaching. They looked prosperous and well-dressed. The man had a distinguished short grey beard, was wearing a dark overcoat and a silk top hat, and leaned heavily on a black cane. His wife's coat was trimmed with fur and her hat, perched on her carefully dressed silver hair, was crowned with imitation flowers and fruit. Mr Holmes took stock of them with a swift glance, instantly calculating who they were and what they wanted, then stood aside to let them enter before going on his way.

"Mr Elliot! Jack!" the elderly man called. "May we come in?"

Mr Elliot stared at them as though he had seen two ghosts.

"Sir Charles!" he exclaimed. "Lady Fleming. What are you doing here?"

"We saw the newspapers, and made enquiries of the police. They told us where you were."

"What do you want? Why have you come?"

"To say sorry," Sir Charles said. "For all the pain we have caused you."

"To ask your forgiveness," Lady Fleming added. "And try to make amends. It is time to heal old wounds." She looked at the youngsters around the table and asked, "Which one is my granddaughter?"

❊   ❊   ❊

Back at HQ that night, the Boys could hardly stop talking about the events of the day. Sherlock Holmes's revelations about what Marvin and Moriarty had been up to were exciting, but the sudden arrival of Mary's grandparents and their reconciliation with her father had made them all think of their own lost families. Several of them had found it hard to hold back their tears.

Sir Charles and Lady Fleming had offered to look after Mary, but Mr Elliot had told them he had no need of their money – the explosion that had nearly killed him in his mine, he said, had uncovered a rich seam of gold. He had made his fortune, and was now wealthier than they were. He would take care of Mary himself, but he would be more than happy for her to see them regularly, and to stay with them on their country estate whenever she wanted to.

Mary had begged the Boys to go and live with her and her father, and Mr Elliot had agreed to look after them all. But they had thanked him and refused: how could they possibly leave HQ and Baker Street and all their adventures? And in any case, what would Mr Holmes do without them? So they had said their farewells. Mary had said a special goodbye to Sparrow, giving him a huge hug and a kiss on the cheek. This time he had not pulled away, or even blushed. But he had shed a quiet tear, and so had several of the others, as Mary promised never to forget them.

With all this buzzing around in their heads, the Boys at first found it hard to get to sleep. But eventually tiredness won, and the only sound to be heard in HQ was heavy breathing. When he thought everyone else was asleep, Beaver dug out his notebook and pencil, and sat down at the table to start writing.

After a few minutes, Queenie crept from her bed, tiptoed over to him and peeped over his shoulder. "What you gonna call it this time?" she whispered.

"Dunno for sure. How about 'The Case of the Captive Clairvoyant'?"

"Yeah," said Queenie. "That'll do. I think that'll do very nicely."